Precious Memories

Blueberry Beach Book Four

Jessie Gussman

Published By: Jessie Gussman

Contents

Acknowledgments

Cover art by Julia Gussman
Editing by Heather Hayden
Narration by Jay Dyess
Author Services by CE Author Assistant

Listen to the unabridged audio for FREE performed by Jay Dyess on the Say with Jay channel on YouTube. Get early access to all of Jay's recordings and listen to Jessie's books before they're available to the general public, plus get daily Bible readings by

Jay and bonus scenes by becoming a Say with Jay channel member.

Chapter 1

Laura Wilson delicately dipped her tiny paintbrush into the small pool of black paint in the little container on her work desk.

For the last fifteen minutes, she had been trying to ignore the pounding music coming from overhead.

No. That was not true.

It wasn't hard for her to ignore the pounding music, which really didn't bother her. It was her grandfather's irritated scowls, muttered words, and jerky movements which had been getting worse and worse that had really been bothering her.

She shifted in her seat, holding the paintbrush still while she did.

Each piece of the handmade, handcrafted, personalized wooden doll people had to be perfectly done, with attention to the minutest detail.

It was what made her grandfather's shop in Blueberry Beach famous all over the eastern United States.

If her grandfather ever got set up online, he could be famous all over the world.

Her grandfather muttered again, growling, and stood up from his stool where he was working on carving the details of the latest miniature piece he was creating.

She was not as good of a carver as her grandfather, but she was a better painter.

The familiar heavy, lead feeling settled deep in her chest, and she fought the temptation to lay her head on her desk.

The exhaustion that she'd been fighting since shortly after her husband cheated on her and left was taking hold.

Carefully cleaning her brush and putting the lid back on the small container of expensive paint, she stood wearily and looked at the clock.

Just ten AM.

Alessandra and Grace were still in school, in third and first grades respectively, and they wouldn't be home for another five hours.

It felt like the morning had already lasted forever, but no matter how short it had been in reality, Laura needed a nap.

The stress from waiting on the possible eruption from her grandfather was far worse than the thumping of the music and occasional banging on the floor. It sounded like the new tenant had his volume maxed out and was dancing with fifty of his friends directly above them.

The vibrations actually were a little bit of a problem. The work they were doing was very exact and needed to be just right.

But her grandfather had always been easily irritated and prone to eruptions. His shop, Blueberry Beach Doll Shop, might not have been the best place for her to come to rest and recover, but it was the only place she could think of. She hadn't wanted to raise her children in the city anyway, and Blueberry Beach was perfect for kids.

Her grandfather picked up a stack of papers then slammed them down with a sharp slap and another growl.

It was funny, seeing how he was almost deaf anyway, that the noise would even bother him. Half the time when she spoke with him, he didn't hear what she said, but apparently, he could hear every note of the music. Or every drumbeat, since there didn't seem to be too many notes.

She chuckled to herself as she wiped her hands down her apron, then untied it and laid it over the back of her chair.

She had trained as a classical cellist but was very grateful that she'd also taken business classes in college, graduating with a dual major, since her classical music training had never earned her a full-time wage.

It just made her a music snob. She sighed, straining her shoulders then taking a step and putting a hand on her desk.

"Grandfather?" she said, trying to infuse confidence in her voice.

When she was younger, he could intimidate her. Now that she was older...he still could. But she tried to pretend he couldn't.

Her grandfather grunted. She took that as a, "What?" and continued. "I'm going to go upstairs and speak to your new tenant.

I'm sure he doesn't realize how his music carries."

She hadn't actually seen the new tenant. Her grandfather had taken care of signing the lease and all that while she had been busy with her children a week ago.

She hadn't been out much, because of her exhaustion, and the man had managed to move in without her ever running into him.

She did know that it was a man, because of what her grandfather said, and she assumed he was an older gentleman, with no children, although she couldn't specifically remember Grandfather saying that.

If she had all of her old energy, she would have been in touch with her friends here in Blueberry Beach, especially Anitra and Zoriah, when she'd moved back to town.

As it was, she hadn't even made it to the diner.

"He's going to get kicked out if he doesn't keep that stuff turned down. How's a man supposed to work when he can't hear himself think!" her grandfather said roughly, his irritation obvious in his choppy movements and the set of his bristled jaw.

"I'm sure he doesn't mean to, Grandfather," Laura said, unwilling to agree to repeat her grandfather's words to the man upstairs.

A particularly loud thump echoed through the small store. Just after that, the bell above the door rang, announcing customers.

Her grandfather turned toward the doorway that led into the shop showroom, which was quite small although beautifully arranged.

Normally, her grandfather was very nice and an actual grandfatherly type, and she always appreciated his words of wisdom, of which he had many.

But when he was irritated, like he was now, his temper seemed to be something he couldn't control.

"I need to see to the customers," Grandfather said, his words slightly modulated as he seemed to gather himself and put on his salesman persona before heading toward the front doorway while Laura turned toward the back.

Her grandfather had been very patient with her exhaustion and her constant need for naps and the fact that she didn't put in a full eight hours every day. More like four.

Of course, he could double his output now that she was here since she could do almost everything he could. The position she filled wasn't one that just anyone could do, although in the summer, he could often get art students from college to do some of the less detailed work.

Often, he had out-of-work artists working for him, but an artist couldn't really make a living in Blueberry Beach, and they soon left.

Laura moved down the hallway toward the back stairs. She and her grandfather lived behind the shop, where he had a kitchen, dining room, and living area, plus the up-stairs which was separated into three bedrooms on one side and the tiny, two-bedroom apartment she was going to visit now on the other. The quarters were small and cramped, and if she was going to stay in Blueberry Beach, she really should find a place of her own.

She couldn't think about that, because she had no idea what she was going to do and no energy to try to come up with something.

Pausing at the bottom of the steps to take several breaths and to tell herself that she could do it, she tried to push aside the exhaustion that made her limbs feel like lead and her body feel like standing alone took superhuman effort.

The idea of climbing the stairs was almost too much. She closed her eyes and said a quick prayer, and then lifted her foot and focused on taking one step at a time. She was out of breath by the second step, but she made it to the top.

Doctors had not been able to figure out what was wrong with her and had finally just diagnosed stress.

Having her husband cheat and leave, then losing her job and severe worry about the custody of her kids—which had turned out to be for naught—had emotionally devastated her, and she supposed what she was experiencing was a nervous breakdown in old-fashioned language.

The doctors had simply advised her to rest and keep her life as stress-free as possible.

She'd also tried to eat healthy and do something normal, even if it was working for her grandfather. At least she was working. At least with Grandfather, she could pretty much set her own hours.

Reaching the top of the stairs, she stood on the landing, giving herself a minute to catch her breath.

She didn't wait long before knocking on the door. The sooner she got this over with, the sooner she could go lie down.

Not that she was sleepy, and she probably wouldn't sleep. She was just...exhausted.

She had to knock three times before the music abruptly shut off, and shortly after that, the door yanked open.

Wherever she'd gotten the idea that the new tenant was an older gentleman had been wrong.

That was her first thought as a large, athletic-looking man scowled down at her.

His t-shirt bulged over a big chest and biceps, and his tanned face held a sheen of sweat. His athletic shorts stopped at his knees, revealing firm calves. He wore the fanciest-looking athletic shoes she'd ever seen.

He was the kind of man she'd always tried to avoid, and he was just her age if she was any judge.

There might have been a little bit of gray at his temples, and his face looked weatherworn, his eyes wise if surprised and slightly narrowed, as though wondering what in the world would make her interrupt him.

Of course, avoiding this kind of man and marrying Christian, her ex, who was the opposite of everything this man was, hadn't worked out too well for her, either.

Christian had been shy and serious with a distinct lack of confidence. Laura had been attracted to him, she had to admit, mostly because of the fact that no one else would be. She wouldn't have to worry about sharing or about him leaving her or not appreciating her.

Of course, when she'd helped him build his business, and he'd become extremely successful, all that had changed, and he'd been pretty quick to find other women who would stroke his ego and do his work, and eventually, he'd dropped Laura.

Loyalty. She should have looked for a man with loyalty.

Maybe that made her wiser, but it didn't make her any more eager to jump back into a relationship with anyone.

She put everything she had into her marriage and into the business they built together, where basically they'd developed ways for people to pay vendors online and sold software that went along with that. They'd made a lot of money, but she'd been blind to the fact that her husband had become less like the man she married and more like the men she had avoided for the very reason of what had happened to her.

Never again.

Chapter 2

"**Y**ou lost?" The man in front of Laura said, giving her a dismissive up-and-down glance that made her feel like she was insignificant and unimportant.

"I'm the granddaughter of your landlord," she said coolly, channeling the business person that she used to be before her world had blown up and she'd become a shell of her former self. "He's busy with a customer currently, but I came up for him. We can hear your music through the floor. The thumping and bumping going on is extremely distracting to us as we work and to him as he tries to wait on customers. We're asking for you to turn your music down and to stop the bumping and thumping."

Even just talking for that amount of time made her out of breath, and she panted a little.

She couldn't be more different than this man in front of her. And it wasn't just his head-banging music with no tone or melody and her with her classical training and love of music that he surely found as distasteful as she found his. His athletic build spoke of obvious care about exercise and endurance, and she could hardly climb the steps and was panting by the second one.

And him with his gruff exterior reminded her more of her grandfather than anyone, and she had always been a people pleaser.

So much for hoping that she might have a neighbor to chat with or someone who she might want to hang out in the shop with and possibly get to know him.

The guy ran a big, blunt hand over his short hair and looked a little abashed. "I'm sorry. Where I lived just before here, I never had to think about how loud my music was. But I do know it can be irritating. I'm sorry. I was thoughtless."

Okay. The guy just rose up several notches in her estimation, because he could apologize.

In her experience, men seldom, if ever, apologized. Even when confronted head-on with things that were most definitely their fault.

She blinked and looked again at this man who didn't hesitate to apologize when he knew he was wrong.

She'd been hasty in her judgment and un-kind, and probably she should apologize.

She shook her head. "I'm sorry. My grand-father was getting a little irritated... He's usually very nice, and sweet and wise, but he has his buttons, I guess."

The guy huffed a breath out, shifting and leaning against the doorjamb. "I guess we all do. I know I do."

She liked that too. Empathy. "Thank you for being so understanding."

"No problem. I'll make sure my music stays low, and I'll try not to exercise up here anymore."

Immediately, she felt bad. It was his home, where else was he to go?

"I'm sorry. I didn't mean to kick you out of your house. Since Devin passed away and his gym closed, that's something Blueberry Beach could really use."

The guy's brows lifted, as though interested, then they kind of lowered and he looked away and blinked, completely dismissing his thought, whatever it was. "You're not kicking me out. There's a whole beach I can exercise on, at least this time of year."

"Yeah. Winters are brutal here. We often get lake-effect snow that buries us until spring."

"So you're a native?"

She nodded with a little, tired smile. "I am. I graduated from Blueberry High, then moved away, and now I'm back for a while."

That was the truth. She didn't know how long "a while" was. A couple of weeks until the girls finished the school year at least, since she could hardly move them to another different school this year. That wouldn't be fair to them with all the upheaval that had been in their lives lately with their father leaving. Although she'd tried to keep all the nasty details of everything that he'd done away from them, they still knew Daddy wasn't living with them anymore. And hadn't been for almost a year. Then of course there was their mother losing her job, as her husband gave it to the woman he'd left her for.

She would have quit anyway. She couldn't work with a man who couldn't be honest.

"I guess you know then that I'm not."

"I knew I didn't recognize you, but you could be a good bit younger or older than me." She tried to say that diplomatically, because she felt like if he was anything, he was older, but knowing how sensitive people, women especially, could be about their age, she didn't say anything. In her experience, men weren't that sensitive, but everyone was different. And she hadn't experienced everything.

His lips quirked up a little, as though seeing her attempt at diplomacy and laughing at it.

"I'm not afraid to say my age," he said with a glint in his eye. "But only if it's reciprocated."

"Then you better keep it a secret," she said, and although she supposed her return held far more flirt than it had in years to any man who wasn't her husband, she didn't really mean it that way. She meant it in the way that said, I'm not the slightest bit interested, leave me alone.

"I'm forty-two," he said, ignoring her words—and his own, apparently, since he'd claimed he wasn't going to tell her how old he was, and then he just did. "And I'm not a native." His bluster seemed to fade a little as his eyes went to the side. "I'm not actually sure what I'm doing here."

The comment surprised her, and she couldn't help her widening eyes and wrinkled brow. "You don't know?"

He lifted his shoulder and looked a little sheepish, like he knew his words were not normal. "Just felt like the Lord wanted me here." He huffed. "I know. For years, I would have laughed at anyone who said that, but I finally figured out that it's a lot better for me if I try to do what the Lord wants rather than what I want. I can't say it's maybe monetarily successful, but I've definitely had better results."

She nodded, not really understanding exactly what he was saying, although she understood being led by the Lord. If she'd allowed the Lord to lead her, she would never have married Christian.

"You seem like you're ex-military," she said, surprised at herself, since she wouldn't usually make such a personal statement.

"Bingo. I am, although nothing big. I was just in the Army right out of high school for three years. Didn't reenlist and couldn't get out of there fast enough. Having people over me all the time telling me what to wear, where to live, what to do down to what to eat and what I could do in my free time... No thank you."

She nodded, envying the casual way he leaned his shoulder on the doorjamb. She was tired and feeling short of breath. She was going to have to leave, even though the little bit that she'd learned about this man made her more curious.

"I suppose I could ask my grandfather what your name is," she said, holding her hand out. "But let me introduce myself, which I should have done to begin with. I'm Laura."

Her fingers were long and slender, and she had been told she had big hands for a woman of her size. She held out her bow hand, and those fingers weren't as dexterous as the ones on her left which were the ones that actually ran across the strings of her cello, grabbing notes and adding vibrance and depth and warmth to the music in the form of vibrato as she played.

Still, she couldn't help but notice the differences in their hands as his took hers. His was brown and thick and strong, and hers was white and slender and delicate.

"Dwane Hardy, ma'am. It's good to meet you, even if you won't tell me how old you are."

"I don't think you really want to know," she said as she shook his hand, more to put him off than anything, although she supposed she could be accused of flirting again. She didn't realize how it would sound until after the words were out of her mouth. "And it's a pleasure to meet you as well. I'm sorry I began our conversation in such an annoyed tone. I appreciate you being gracious with my request."

"It was reasonable, and I was inconsiderate." His words were firm. She admired that confidence. It reminded her of her own, back when she used to have it.

"I should have been more gracious. If you ever need anything, I live with my grandfather and my two daughters in the rooms in the back behind the store. You're certainly welcome there anytime." Her grandfather had always been hospitable, which was another reason why she didn't hesitate to move in with him. He was a good man, if a bit short tempered on occasion.

"Well, maybe you better tell me all the things that I could possibly do that would irritate him before I make an appearance. I don't want to upset anyone."

"I'm sorry. He's really a good man."

"That's the impression I got when we met about the lease. I thought maybe I was wrong in my assessment."

"No. But I suppose anything that gets between him and putting out a superior quality product irritates him. The loud music made it difficult for him to concentrate, and the vibrations made it difficult to do the detailed work that he needs to."

"So you're saying he makes all those little figurines that are in the store?"

Chapter 3

"You were in the store?" Laura asked before she realized it was a stupid question. He probably had been when he met with her grandfather. She had never had too much to do with the tenants that lived above them. When she and her sisters lived with their grandfather from the time she was in fifth grade until she graduated from high school, there had just been one tenant, an older gentleman who kept to himself most of the time. "I'm sorry. Of course you were. That's probably where you signed your lease contract," she said, turning and moving away until her back met the wall of the small landing. Her hand rested on the wood railing.

"I should have asked you in," Dwane said, pausing before saying, "You're welcome to come in." She felt like he really meant it.

She shook her head. "I need to go."

"You work in the store?" he asked, ignoring her statement.

"Yes. With my grandfather."

"You carve the figures? They're all hand carved?" he asked, wonder in his voice.

"I can. Although my grandfather's better at carving. I mostly paint, and I'm better at that than he is." It wasn't bragging. It was true.

"Man. I had no idea they were all carved and painted by hand. All those little figurines in the houses...there was so much detail in them. Tables and chairs and beds and I even saw a little refrigerator and microwave. Hard to believe all the stuff they had, but I never thought for one minute that they were handcrafted."

"That's what makes it special. A person can bring in a picture of their family, and Grandfather will carve them figurines based on the features that they have, and then I paint them to the same specs."

"Wow. I've never heard of that. That's quite a personalized item and would make a great gift."

"Actually, that's what I was working on today. Something that is going to be a gift for this Christmas."

"Christmas? It's barely May!"

Laura nodded. "It takes a long time to make them, because they're so detailed and authentic. We actually have orders up through the next three years, mostly for Christmas, although some people want them immediately."

"Great heirloom gift. Something the whole family can cherish. I get it," Dwane said, seeming thoughtful. "That's where I saw the most success in my business."

"You have a business?"

"Had one. My partner bought me out, and I probably shouldn't have allowed it, but like I said, I've been allowing the Lord to lead me, and I felt like it was time to move on, even though I was comfortable and making a fantastic living and..." His voice trailed off like there were parts of his life that had not been perfect.

But Laura didn't get the feeling that he was lying, just not saying everything that could be said.

Her hand rested on the banister, the weight of her exhaustion feeling like it could push her down the steps. She needed to get away, but she didn't want to be rude.

"I think it's an admirable thing to leave something that successful just because you feel the Lord's taking you away. But doesn't He usually have a plan and He moves you from one thing to another for a reason? Blueberry Beach seems like a weird place to just come when you don't even have a job?"

Her brain was being sluggish, and she finally figured out that maybe that was what
he was saying.

"No. I don't have anything lined up." He
grinned a little. "I do have money from the
sale of my business. It was quite a lot. So
it's not that I have to work, but I want to. I
don't want to just sit around all day and do
nothing."

She snorted. "Grandfather is always looking for someone to sweep up shavings in
the shop and do odd jobs. If you're good at
waiting on customers, he might have you
do that a little too, although he's very particular and likes to talk to people himself."

"I thought it odd when you called him
Grandfather. But the way you're talking

about him kind of makes me feel like the name suits."

She liked the dimple in his cheek and the way, even though he was large and quite muscular, that he didn't seem threatening to her. Maybe it was just her exhaustion keeping her normal defenses down. Still, there was something about him that made her feel like she was safe.

"It does. And I noticed you're not jumping on the offer to sweep and clean up the shop. Normally, it's something that he gets a teenager from the school to do. But it's been harder and harder to hire kids to work."

"I experienced that in my own business. I'm not sure we're doing kids any favors by keeping them from working when they're younger. But the law is what it is." His voice sounded thoughtful, but then he grinned. "I'll have to talk to your grandfather about a job. I don't know what God has for me, but in the meantime, I'm not afraid to push a broom."

"It must be a step down from owning your own business."

"When you own your business, you do everything. You pick up the slack, fill in the cracks, and do whatever needs to be done. You can't sit around and wait for someone else to do it or look at a job and say 'that's not mine.' Everything's yours. So you just do it."

Laura knew exactly what he was talking about. She owned her business with her husband, except she allowed him to put everything in his name, and she hadn't gotten her fair share out of their divorce settlement.

Of course, she hadn't realized he'd started putting things in his girlfriend's name before she'd found out about their affair.

That's what she got for trusting someone who wasn't trustworthy.

Not information she wanted to go into with the stranger standing in front of her. No matter how nice he seemed and no matter how safe she thought he was.

"I can see how that would be the way it is," she finally said, not wanting to lie but not wanting to hint even a little bit that she had a business with her ex. Not because she was ashamed of it, just because she couldn't stand talking about it right now.

She was supposed to avoid stress and be relaxing and recovering, not rehashing everything in her mind.

Talking about him brought everything back, and she didn't want to go there.

"So you paint for your grandfather. Is that what you've done since you came back from college?" he asked, and she felt like he was just making conversation.

She needed to tell him she had to go. But somehow, her mouth just wouldn't say those words. She supposed it'd been so long since she had a friendly conversation with a man who wasn't an egotistical jerk that she couldn't make herself disengage even though this was a dangerous question.

"No. I guess I was like everyone else. I left my hometown for a while, thinking there were bigger and better things."

Looking back, she had felt vaguely dissatisfied with everything long before she found out about her husband's affair. Maybe someday, she could say that her husband's affair was the best thing that ever happened to her. Not today.

"And I found out what I have here: community, friends, a shop that's loved and respected and that blesses people, work that is fulfilling, and a great place to raise my daughters, and I don't know why I ever moved away and thought it was a good idea."

"What age are your daughters?" he said, his tone neutral.

"I have one in first grade and one in third."

"That's nice." He ran a hand over his head. His face shut down, and she was pretty sure the conversation was over. Maybe she should have been offended or perhaps relieved, but she was just grateful she would finally be able to go lie down.

"It was nice chatting with you," he said, straightening out from the doorjamb and jerking his chin at her.

"I'm sure we'll see each other around, although I haven't been out much. I suppose that's why we haven't met."

"We'll definitely be seeing each other if your grandfather hires me in the shop, right? You do work in the shop?"

"In the back. If he hires you, you'll probably mostly be working out front with customers and doing a lot of dusting and cleaning."

"I look forward to seeing you again."

She wanted to say something along those lines back to him, but her mouth just kinda froze, and the weight that had been pushing her down for so long, heavy and hard and black inside of her, maybe didn't succeed, exactly, but it managed to knock her off balance as she turned toward the stairs, and her hand just didn't have the strength to grab onto the banister. She ended up smacking her head off the wood railing and rolling down the stairs.

It would have been nice to lose consciousness. That way she would be less embarrassed and sore and exhausted.

Dwane was beside her almost instantly as she landed at the bottom of the stairs. That was the one thing she was sure of; the rest of the world seemed a little dizzy.

Lately, dizziness wasn't uncommon when she lay down in bed. The world would spin sometimes before it stopped when she was feeling this exhausted. But she'd never had dizziness be a problem that would make her lose her balance and fall like she just had.

"Are you okay? Don't move. You might have a back injury."

"I'm okay. I just basically rolled down the stairs. At least it wasn't head over heels."

"If you have a back injury, moving will make it worse."

"I wouldn't be able to move, right?" she said slowly, her face knit together, her thoughts in a jumble. And honestly, she just wished Dwane would leave so she could gather herself up and go collapse in bed.

"I'm going to call 911."

"Don't," she said, some of her old confidence and command coming back into her voice, making him freeze with his hand halfway to the phone in his back pocket.

"Are you sure?"

"I think I just need to lie down for a bit."

"I'll carry you to wherever you need to go." Then he huffed and looked away. "I don't want to push in. But I will. I feel bad that you fell and I didn't catch you."

"No one expected you to."

"That doesn't mean I shouldn't have."

"I think I can get up." She started pulling herself together, twisting, and fighting the exhaustion that said just stay right there. "I think I could lie on this floor forever," she muttered.

"Please don't."

She rolled to her side and up on her elbow, but she stopped, panting. It was a relief when she felt his arms go under her knees and around her shoulders, and he picked her up.

Maybe she should have been impressed at how easily he did it, but she wasn't really thinking about that. Rather, she guided him to the door, which he opened after he adjusted her in his arms and followed her directions to the couch, depositing her on it and standing up.

"Can I get you a glass of water?"

"No. Honest. I'm fine. I know it's weird to have someone fall down the stairs. I do have some medical issues, but nothing that's going to hurt me. I appreciate your help. You can go."

It was a dismissal, and she hoped he understood that. As nice as he was, it was embarrassing to be less than her best, and she was almost too exhausted to speak.

With a last look at her, he jerked his head. "I'm gonna scribble my number on the notepad on your refrigerator. If you need me, give me a call."

"Thank you," she said, grateful that she could just lie without moving and was done having to talk as well, although she was frustrated because she didn't want to be weak. She didn't want to be so tired she couldn't do anything. She wanted to be up and moving, active and engaged with her life, and not waste it lying around unable to move.

Lord, I'd really like to get better. Please.

Chapter 4

Dwane shifted in the small living room, barely noticing the worn furniture, or the off-white walls, or the cotton curtains in the window.

He wanted to call 911, wanted to at the very least take her in to the ER himself, but she had specifically said no.

It had been ingrained in him to respect a person's "no."

Of course, he'd carried her, and she hadn't exactly given permission.

He shifted, careful not to bump the small coffee table that sat in front of the couch, as he watched the woman, Laura, lie with her eyes closed, her face pale, and her body unmoving except for a shallow rise and fall of her chest.

Surely if she were a diabetic, she would have said something. He could have gotten her a glass of juice or a candy bar.

He couldn't think of anything else that he could help with that would have caused her to...get dizzy? Black out? What, exactly, had happened?

He would have said she just lost her balance, except, thinking back on it, she had been acting a little...weak.

"Did you have breakfast?" he asked, softly, in case she was sleeping, although he was pretty sure she hadn't fallen immediately to sleep in the sixty seconds he'd been standing there trying to figure out what to do.

His conscience wouldn't let him just leave her.

"I did. I promise, I'm fine." Her words were soft and weak but still firm, leaving no room for argument.

"I'll let your grandfather know what happened." Her head jerked, and he warded off whatever protest she was going to utter. "I'm not calling 911, and I'm not taking you to the ER, but I am going to tell your grandfather."

Her hand twitched, like she was giving up. Her face seemed to relax a little.

"Thanks for caring for me," she said again, her eyes never opening.

He strode out, determined to say something to her grandfather, although he felt like he was about five years old and tattling on his younger siblings.

He walked down the hall, then let himself in the back room. A desk with neatly closed paint jars sat just slightly off-center in the room, and he assumed that was probably where Laura worked.

She seemed like a nice lady, although she had been carefully clear that she was not interested in a romantic relationship, and he felt like that could possibly be a good thing, since they could be friends without any expectations.

Before he reached the doorway, he could see that her grandfather, Gavin, was still dealing with a customer. He walked in anyway, moving off to the side so as not to disturb them and putting his hands behind his back, careful not to touch anything.

Now that he knew that every piece was hand carved, and many of them one of a kind, along with hand-painted, he felt like they were much more expensive than what he had originally thought when he was in the shop the first time.

Then, they just looked like figurines that might be available anywhere. Although wooden figurines were becoming rare. Most of the time, they were plastic or ceramic and made with a mold.

The years he'd spent in business, even though his business had nothing to do with this, had him calculating how much it must cost to make each set, and each individual piece, and wondering if there was much profit in it.

He examined them closely, bending down and marveling at the minute attention to detail that each piece showed.

Laura's slender hands came to mind as he noticed the careful lines of paint, the eyes, which even had eyelashes and brows. Amazing. He would love to watch her work, since the attention to detail and the talent and skill it must take to do what she did was almost incomprehensible.

The carving, too, was incredibly skilled, and his hands itched a little as he kept them behind his back. Almost like they wanted to try it for themselves.

He'd never done anything of that sort and could hardly imagine he'd be any good at it, but he could see himself loving work like that, which would surprise anyone who knew him since he was an active guy, and the businesses that he'd owned with his friend had been athletic clubs and gyms which had suited him perfectly.

Unfortunately, his friend wanted to expand in ways he didn't want to, and while they parted on friendly terms, he sometimes wished he hadn't felt forced to sell.

Still, there was a peace about being in Blueberry Beach that he wouldn't trade for anything. This was where he needed to be.

Being in the shop also felt peaceful and right, and he wondered at that feeling, which was an unnatural one for him. Not one he'd felt often in his life.

The door jingled, and he looked up to realize that the customers that Gavin had been talking to had just left.

He'd been so deep in thought, so awed by the workmanship before him, that he hadn't even noticed.

"My granddaughter talked to you?" Gavin said from beside him.

"She did, Gavin. I wanted to come in and apologize. I hadn't considered how thin the walls were and that your shop was right below me. I should have, and I'm sorry."

Some people had a problem with apologizing, but he supposed he didn't really understand it. If a person was wrong, what was the harm in saying so?

Gavin's stern expression eased a little under the heavy white whiskers. He nodded his head. "I appreciate the apology. I hope she wasn't too hard on you?"

Seemed like there was a twinkle in Gavin's eyes as he said those words, and Dwane felt himself responding as his face relaxed into almost a grin.

"She wasn't. She's just a little thing anyway," he said, realizing it was true. He had noticed how much smaller she was than him, but standing here in the shop, he felt huge, while Laura would fit right in.

"She's little, but she's tough."

There was no mistaking the pride in Gavin's voice as he talked about his granddaughter. His words reminded Dwane of what he had determined to say.

"She fell down the stairs. She claims there's nothing wrong, but I had to carry her into your living room and lay her on the couch. I was worried about her, but she wouldn't allow me to call an ambulance or take her to the ER myself."

Maybe there was a little bit of alarm in Gavin's eyes as he listened, but then his head nodded sagely. "She's been struggling with something, not life-threatening, but something that might make her fall down the stairs. She's not hurt?" he asked, his voice maybe a touch more gruff, which Dwane assumed to be emotion—concern and maybe a little fear—for his granddaughter.

The man might be old and a little crusty, but he cared about her. That eased Dwane's mind more than anything.

"She claims not to be. I couldn't see anything, and she was able to move all of her limbs okay. Just..." He ran a hand over his hair, hooking it behind his neck. He wasn't good with all the gushy feelings, but he wanted to make sure her grandfather knew everything. "She's just lying there so still and white. I mean, she didn't even open her eyes when she was talking to me. She didn't move at all after I laid her down. It didn't seem natural."

None of that seemed to surprise Gavin who just nodded. "That's normal for her, for now anyway."

It made him think that maybe she was a little different at one time.

It surprised him that he was curious. But he found he really was. He wished he'd had more time to talk to her. He hadn't wanted to let her go when she said she needed to.

Maybe that was what caused the fall. Maybe she knew she was getting weak, and he had wanted to continue their conversation and hadn't allowed her to leave.

The thought made him feel guilty, but it was a guilt he couldn't do anything about, so he ignored it.

He hadn't really planned to say anything more, but the words just flowed out of his mouth. "She said you might be hiring. She said I might be able to get a job here."

The money that he made from his partner, cash, not including the stocks and company shares he'd been given, had left him so that he was sitting comfortably. He didn't need to work.

But this felt right.

He didn't typically make decisions with his feelings, but this feeling said he was right where the Lord wanted him to be, and he'd better stay put. What better way to stay put than to get a job working here?

"I typically hire a teenager to sweep the floor and clean up and wait on customers if I can't get up to take care of sales, and if they're very trustworthy, I might allow them to package and ship merchandise as well." Gavin tilted his head and looked Dwane up and down. "Is that the kind of work you're interested in?"

Dwane nodded easily. "I'm willing to do that. But I'd also like to learn to carve."

That surprised the old man. His brows shot up, and his head moved back, while his eyes narrowed. "I've been doing it for seventy years, and I'm still learning. It takes a lot of patience and a lot of time, and you can't get in a rush."

"I have more patience now than I used to. And I'm developing more every day. As for time…" He shrugged. "I have plenty."

Gavin nodded his head thoughtfully, as though weighing his words and thinking about what Dwane had said. Finally, he said, "We'll start you on sweeping the floor, keeping the shelves neat, and handling customers. We'll see how it goes and go from there. I'm not making any promises, but I've been thinking for a while now it's time for me to start training someone else to take my place. Although Laura is a pretty good carver. With practice, she could be great."

"I don't want to take her job or position if carving is what she wants," Dwane said immediately. That was a no-brainer. He wasn't here to step on anyone's toes, least of all the woman in the back room, lying on the couch, with something, he didn't know what, but something, that wasn't quite right with her.

"You don't need to worry about that. Laura doesn't mind carving, but painting is really where she shines, and that's what she loves. She is the opposite of me."

"You can paint okay, but you love carving?" Dwane guessed when Gavin didn't say anything more.

"That's right. I think that's probably true about most people. We all have an area where we are really good, then we're semi-decent in other ways."

Dwane thought maybe people had more than one area that they were really good in, but perhaps they just found one and stuck with that and never realized that they could be good at other things.

"When would you like me to start?" he asked, not having plans other than to exercise daily. He wanted to spend more time at the beach too. What was the point of living in a beach town if one didn't enjoy the beach?

He'd been there several times, but with getting everything moved in, and settled, and getting the place stocked with groceries, he hadn't taken the time to do more than walk down twice.

"Whenever you want to. I have paperwork to fill out—it's online now—so I have all your legal stuff online, and we have a payroll service." Gavin went on to give a few more details about the job, which of course did not include any benefits and included more hours in the summer than in the winter, at which time he might possibly be laid off.

It was May, and winter seemed like a long way away; who knew what the Lord would have him doing by then. He nodded and followed Gavin to the back, where a computer he hadn't noticed before sat on a small counter.

"I'll get this up for you, then if you don't mind, I'm going to go back and check on Laura. She will be fine, but I want to check. And..." The man paused, his fingers stilling as he clicked into the computer. Finally, he said, "Her health is hers, and I guess she'll tell you what she wants you to know. And I suppose if you're working here, you'll see her."

That was all he said, and it didn't exactly soothe Dwane's uneasiness. In fact, it inflamed more.

So there really was something wrong with her, something that he would notice when working with her.

He shouldn't be that interested. He wasn't sure why he cared, but he did.

Still, he didn't say anything, just nodded, waiting for Gavin to get the right screen up on the computer, then he stepped in, filling out the employment form to basically be the custodian of a small beachside shop. If only his friends could see him now.

Chapter 5

aura sat, paintbrush in hand, trying to ignore the man who swept up shavings just a few feet away.

Normally, they didn't sweep while she was working, because of the dust and the potential for it to get airborne then stick on the paint and ruin the finish. But her grandfather had shown Dwane how to sweep gently and pull just the shavings up to make the floor less slippery. That's what he was doing now.

It had been a week since she found out her grandfather had hired him, and she kicked herself for even mentioning the idea to

Dwane when they were talking. What had possessed her?

Of course, at the time she hadn't considered how awkward it would be to be in the little shop with someone so large. He seemed to take all of the space in the room and all of the air too. He'd only been there a couple of days before her grandfather had decided to give him a chance to carve.

Nothing important, of course. As her grandfather said, it was only to see if he had the ability to translate what his eyes saw into his hands.

Her grandfather had said the same thing about her and her sisters when they were younger.

It turned out Laura was the only one that had that elusive thing. Whatever her grandfather was talking about.

Apparently, her grandfather had decided that Dwane had it too, because for the last four nights, after the shop closed in the evening and after they'd had supper, her grandfather had met with Dwane in the back shop, teaching him about carving.

It would take a long time until Dwane could produce anything that might be sellable, but her grandfather must have decided that he would be able to eventually since he was spending his time with him.

"I'm going to run down to the diner for some lunch. Do you want anything?" Dwane asked as he gently slid the shavings into the garbage can, then put the broom and dustpan away.

"Thank you, but I'm fine." She willed her hands to be steady as she looked up at him, still not completely comfortable. Maybe it was embarrassment over the way they met, but it was more than likely be-cause men like Dwane, big and muscular, confident and athletic, had always made her nervous.

She wasn't sure why. He certainly wasn't threatening. In any way.

"Let me know if you change your mind." He seemed to look at her just a little longer than strictly necessary before he walked out.

He made her nervous and uncomfortable, but there was something about him that made her curious too. Or, if it were possible to be nervous and uncomfortable but also confident that if he needed to protect her, he would, there was that.

Basically, her feelings for the new hire/new tenant didn't make any sense.

The bell jingled from the outer shop as he walked out, and her grandfather's voice drifted in as he spoke with a customer.

It would get a lot busier once school was out and people started coming to the beach for the day. Weekends especially would be crazy, and Dwane's help would really come in handy.

He'd been willing to do anything they'd ask him to, from cleaning the shelves to waiting on customers to boxing things up and shipping them out, which her grandfather didn't usually allow just anyone to do.

She wasn't irritated by the way her grandfather had almost instantly trusted Dwane. It actually made her even more curious. Because her grandfather was typically a pretty good judge of character, although usually it took him a bit to make up his mind.

"Knock knock?" A woman's voice made her head jerk up.

Laura had to stare for a moment before recognition hit her. "Zoriah?" She said the name slowly with suppressed excitement.

Zoriah nodded. "You recognize me!"

"You haven't changed at all. You look as young as you did the last time I saw you…what…at the end of the summer of our senior year?"

"Probably. I don't remember seeing you after that. That's too nice of you to say though. I definitely feel a lot older. A lot of water under the bridge."

"I think that's the case with everyone." Laura dipped her paintbrush in the water beside her and screwed the cap on her paint. "Come on in and sit down. Do you have time to chat?"

"I was hoping you did," Zoriah said, although instead of sitting down at the other desk, she came over and put her arms around Laura. "It's been so long. I can't believe how the years have flown."

"Me either. We should have stayed in touch."

"I think everyone says that. We get busy, and things happen." Her eyes looked Laura up and down. "You're skinnier than I remember."

"That's a good thing, right?" Laura said, trying to make her lips smile. A person was pretty tired when they were too tired to eat.

"I've heard that you're not well," Zoriah said slowly, "but I don't want to pry. Although, I'm asking because I don't want to wear you out either." She settled into Grandfather's large chair.

"You heard correctly. The doctors say there's nothing wrong, just a combination of stress and all the things that have happened have given me exhaustion, I guess."

"They can't diagnose you with anything?"

Laura shook her head. "No. And there's no treatment other than to avoid stress and eat right. Beyond that, they don't really have any suggestions."

"But they ruled some things out?"

"I think they ruled everything out. I can't imagine there being more medical tests available than the number of tests I was subject to over the last year."

"Oh, that's terrible. I hate going to the hospital lab."

"Me too. It's like a torture chamber that you actually pay to get tortured in."

They laughed, then Zoriah said, "I'm sorry I haven't visited before this."

"It's okay. I haven't been out much. I should've gone to see you. I've just been...tired."

"I totally understand."

"I heard you had a store, though? You opened up your grandmother's clothing shop again?"

"I was going to, but there were a lot of problems with that, and I ended up opening a secondhand store. Which I love, and I can see my grandmother smiling about. She never said anything about wanting to open that kind of store, but I just don't have a problem picturing her loving it. Which gives me peace."

"Your grandmother was a special lady. And I think you're right, although I would say that whatever you do would have made her happy."

Maybe a sheen of tears misted Zoriah's eyes. "That's a beautiful thought. Thank you." She ran a finger through the dust on the desk. Then she said, "My sister passed away, and I have her children with me."

"I hadn't heard that," Laura said honestly. Surprised. "You have children of your own?"

Zoriah's lips lifted, but she shook her head. "That has never happened for me. God blessed me with my sister's kids. I'd already been spending a lot of time with them, although the role of mother is a lot different than the role of aunt."

"I know. So much different. But they tell me being a grandmother is fun."

"I hope I get to find that out, although Macy and Mark are still in school, and I don't want to find out before they're done with that."

"Of course not."

"So you must not have heard what Macy did?" Zoriah's words were tentative.

"No?"

Something that looked like relief passed over Zoriah's face. "I was afraid, just a little bit, that maybe you'd heard what she'd done and decided it was too risky to be friends with me. Probably I would have been here sooner if I hadn't been afraid of that."

"I can't imagine Macy would have done anything that would make me not want to be friends with you. That's crazy."

"Well, you haven't heard how bad it really was."

And Zoriah proceeded to tell Laura how Macy had vandalized almost all the businesses on Main Street and most of the businesses in Blueberry Beach. Zoriah's store had been one of the ones Macy had left untouched.

It'd been a terrible thing, because as small shop owners, their profit margins were extremely thin, not to mention they were such a tight-knit community, and people had been so nice about helping Zoriah start her secondhand store. She had already felt like she owed them, and then her niece, who was in her custody, had gone and done a terrible thing like that.

Laura could feel the tiredness seeping into her bones, but she got herself out of her chair as Zoriah finished her story, dabbing at the tears that had leaked out of the corners of her eyes, and walked over, putting her arms around her friend and squeezing tightly.

"We try to raise them right, and Macy wasn't even yours. Going through so much with her mother's death. Your grandmother died not that long ago either, right?"

Zoriah nodded. "She'd seen a lot of death. That's true. But it didn't excuse what she did. But the people here were so gracious and forgiving. We didn't deserve it, but it was a beautiful experience for me, and

Macy has completely turned around and has been trying to make everything right as well as paying the fines the judge gave her."

"She wasn't sentenced to jail time?"

"No one would press charges."

"I love our small town. I can't believe I thought it was a good idea to move away. I'm glad I'm back," Laura said, meaning every word.

"Well, gossip is a big thing here, and..." Zoriah looked up.

Laura backed up a little, reaching out for the end of her desk and settling herself back into her chair.

"What?" Laura said, her head tilted.

"I guess we're all concerned about you. You know we know that you're having some health problems, and I hope you don't feel like we're butting in, but I wanted to see if there was anything I could do?"

Chapter 6

It was on the tip of Laura's tongue to tell Zoriah no, she didn't need anything, but she'd had a worry that had been nagging at her for a while, and it now came to the front of her mind.

"I've been concerned about summer coming, and the girls getting out of school, and what I'm going to do with them. I barely have enough energy to work four hours here. Maybe a few more in the afternoon after taking a rest, but I just... I just don't have it in me, right now anyway, and I don't want my girls running wild, especially with all the tourists here. The rest of the year,

Blueberry Beach is as safe as any place, but in the summer…"

Zoriah nodded knowingly. She'd grown up in Blueberry Beach. She knew how the tourist season was and how it made them really appreciate the quietness and peace of the rest of the year. Even while the residents of Blueberry Beach needed tourist money to survive. "I understand." She blinked and bit her lip. "I know everyone will give you a hand in keeping an eye on them. It's so much nicer to have someone you know watching your kids."

Laura nodded with relief. Her kids had been through too much. She didn't want to let them with someone she didn't know and didn't trust. She hadn't figured out what exactly she was going to do.

"Macy has five hundred hours of community service that she has to complete by the end of the summer," Zoriah said thoughtfully, her finger tapping the desk again. "I'll check and see, but...I bet watching your girls would count." Her brows crinkled together, and she bit her lip and put her hand up as though warding off the protests that she was sure was coming.

Laura didn't have any intention of protesting. She waited quietly.

"I know... I know as a mom you're probably concerned because Macy was involved in some pretty bad things. I mean, to do what she did... She was just in a pretty bad place."

Laura wanted to wait and listen, but she wanted to reassure Zoriah more because she couldn't stand seeing her so worried and insecure. "You know how gossip is in a small town. I didn't hear the details of anything that Macy had done. But I have heard that your niece has turned herself around – no details on what the problem was to begin with – and people come in the shop complimenting her all the time. Saying what a great student she is. Or how she's helped people around town, or just what a great employee she is at the ice-cream store."

"Really?"

Laura nodded, completely honest. "Really. I guess I only get bits and pieces of conversations with me sitting in the back here working most of the time, but her name has come up, along with glowing compliments. You really don't need to be concerned. Not about her reputation, with me anyway."

Zoriah took a moment to compose herself, and Laura was glad she had taken the time to say what she had. She supposed a mother never stopped worrying about her children. And it was always a joy and blessing to hear good things about them.

"Well, then maybe it would actually be okay if I can find out if Macy can babysit?" Zoriah still didn't seem completely confident.

"That would be a huge blessing to me. I've been, not worried exactly, because I've been trying not to worry about anything, but I've definitely been wondering what in the world I'm going to do with my children this summer."

"As I remember from your childhood, you lived with your grandfather for a while... Your mom moved around a lot?"

Laura nodded. She hadn't wanted to talk about her family much when she was younger. If anyone thought it odd that she and her sisters lived with her grandfather a good bit of the time, people were usually too polite to say anything.

"She was in and out of relationships. She actually got married, and I thought maybe she was turning everything around, about the time I graduated from high school. But that lasted less than a decade, and it blew up too. Although, the guy she's with now, she's been with for a while. They're not married, but he seems to be good for her."

"I see. I was just wondering because I didn't want to take a grandmother away from her grandchildren, if you felt like you needed to give Macy the hours if she ends up being approved for them."

"No," Laura said with a small laugh. "She's never really been involved in my children's life. Or mine." It might have made things easier if she'd had her mother to fall back on when Christian had dropped his big bombshell on her.

Her sisters had been supportive but not close, since they were scattered all over the country. Still, they had been people she could talk to, and she appreciated it.

Her mother, not so much. There was always drama in her life, and a phone call with her was to hear all about her drama, and by the time she was done, Laura never really felt like talking about her own. Not that her mother seemed interested. She supposed that's just the way some people were.

Sometimes, she wondered what it would be like to actually have a mother who cared. It's the kind of mother she wanted to be to her children, and part of why this exhaustion had been so frustrating. She couldn't be a good mom if all she could do was lie around on the couch.

She couldn't be a good mom if she couldn't even work enough to support her children, feed them, and have a house for them to live in.

She couldn't keep thinking about those things though, because she would get depressed.

"I really hope things work out with Macy. That would solve so many of my problems right now." She sighed. "Not that my children are problems. I didn't mean it like that."

"I know exactly what you mean. They're not problems, but they cause problems. Even though you love them, you don't always love the drama the kids bring into your life."

"So true." Zoriah had said that better than she ever could.

She was opening her mouth to ask how soon Zoriah might know whether Macy could do it or not, just so she had an idea of whether or not she should be looking for...a babysitter? A daycare? Or maybe trying to arrange with her grandfather that he would take care of them in the evenings while she worked and she could take care of them during the day while he did. But the door to the shop opened, and the bells jingled.

From where she sat, she could see Dwane walk in.

She glanced over, knowing that her grandfather's desk was positioned in such a way that Zoriah would be able to see him too.

Sure enough, her eyes were bright, and she had a little grin on her face as she turned to Laura. "Oh! This is your handsome neighbor I've heard so much about. For some reason, he hasn't been in my secondhand shop." That last bit was said with a lot of humor and not a little irony, and Laura smiled with her. As a single man living by himself, Dwane probably didn't have too much reason to be in a secondhand shop. And wouldn't visit her store just for the love of shopping.

"He's cute," Zoriah said after taking another glance at Dwane.

Laura didn't want Dwane to hear. It wasn't that she was afraid that he might know that she thought he was cute. It was more that she was afraid that if he knew that she thought he was cute, he might think that she was interested in more than the uneasy friendship that they seemed to have developed between them.

Friendship she could do. Cute, and the things that came with that, she could not.

She didn't even want to try.

She knew it was kind of cliché to get burned by love and decide that one was never going to love again. But unless it happened to a person, a person really couldn't understand how true it was.

Not to mention, she hadn't just gotten burned by love. She'd lost her health, her job, her stable family, and all the security that she had had about her future.

Everything was gone.

Plus, and this probably broke her heart more than any of the other things put together, her children had lost their father.

Of course, Christian was probably a better father than a lot of men who had left their wives and kids for someone younger and prettier and better suited to him, since he did see them one or two weekends a month.

They hadn't fought over custody. It had just been assumed that she would take care of them, and of course, she was completely fine with that.

She'd been very accommodating, as much as she could, allowing him to see them any time he wanted to.

If the girls cried because Daddy didn't live with them anymore, because Daddy didn't love them, because Daddy left and Mommy must be bad because Daddy left her, well… No one could blame her for not wanting to do the "cute" thing again.

For the protection of her children.

Not just the protection of her own heart and health.

"Hey," Dwane said as he stepped in the back workshop, his eyes glinting as he looked at Laura, then surprise entering them as they moved almost immediately to Zoriah.

He stopped. "I can duck back out. I didn't know I was interrupting something back here." He shifted the bags he held in his hands, and his body moved backward.

"No!" Zoriah said as she jumped up. "We were just chatting, and I need to get back."

"Dwane, this is Zoriah. She owns the secondhand store at the end of the street. We were friends growing up here in Blueberry Beach," Laura said, not standing, although she felt slightly impolite for not. She was just so tired and felt like she should conserve her energy. Even just talking to Zoriah had made her feel wiped out.

"Nice to meet you, Zoriah," Dwane said, shifting the bags and holding out his hand, which Zoriah took and pumped enthusiastically. "I've seen your shop as I've walked down the street heading toward the beach. Looks cute."

There was that word again. For some reason, Laura was tempted to giggle. It was a good thing she was so tired. She might have actually done it.

"Thanks. You'll have to stop in sometime to chat and look around."

"I'll do that." Dwane dropped his hand and shifted the bags again.

"I'm headed back," Zoriah said, turning to look at Laura. "Please don't hesitate to say something if you need anything. And I'll ask and find out about Macy and let you know."

"Thanks. I appreciate it."

With a little wave, Zoriah headed out, and pretty soon, the bells jingled, signaling that she had left the store.

Dwane's eyes shifted around the room awkwardly, as though trying to think of something to say. Normally, they didn't en-gage in much conversation, but normally, she was working and could use concentrating on her painting as an excuse to not.

Her paint was put away, though, along with her brush, and her hands felt empty and useless, and she didn't know what to say.

"I,... Well, I know you said you didn't want anything, but I got something anyway."

Obviously, she wasn't the only one who was nervous or felt like their positions were awkward. Dwane seemed to stumble a good bit with his words as he walked over and set the bag down in front of her.

"I noticed that you eat a lot of peanut butter and jelly, and I thought you might appreciate an actual sandwich. So I got us both one from the hot sausage place down at the end of the street on the boardwalk."

It smelled amazing, now that it was sitting in front of her, and her stomach rumbled. Her appetite had fled along with her energy, and anything that made her stomach rumble was a good thing in her book.

"That was so thoughtful of you. Thank you so much."

"Thoughtful, or maybe I just figured if I got myself one, came back, and ate it in front of you, it'd be rude. If you end up not wanting yours, I'm not too proud to eat what's left."

"Oh? So you wanted two?" Laura was amazed that she actually felt disappointed. Her mouth was watering, and she felt like she really could eat the sandwich.

"No. I got fries along with mine, and that will be more than I should eat. Although I could probably eat two, I shouldn't."

They shared a laugh. "I know what you mean."

"I don't think you do. You look pretty slender."

She didn't want to get into the fact that she had lost thirty pounds in the last year since her husband left her. So she just smiled and shook her head and opened the bag.

"Have you had these before?" she asked him as she pulled her sandwich out, the soft white roll cradling the succulent, steaming sausage dripping with onions and peppers and smelling like heaven in a bun.

"Nope. I passed him several times while he was setting up, but I've never been there when he's actually been open. That's why I made a point today of going out and getting them."

She typically ate a peanut butter and jelly sandwich at her desk if she was at the shop over lunch and not napping. He often ran upstairs to his apartment, and she had no idea what he ate. Which made her think for the first time that maybe he would appreciate it if they shared some meals. She had to cook for her grandfather and daughters anyway...

And there she was, giving herself more work when she was supposed to be resting.

"I haven't been there yet this year, but Carl has had a hot sausage stand here in Blueberry Beach for at least thirty years. Last year, he was talking about retiring, but I don't think he ever will."

"I know how that goes," Dwane said, pulling his own sausage out and using his paper bag as a placemat on her grandfather's desk. "I don't know if this guy's name was Carl. He didn't look as old as the hills, but close."

She laughed. "That's Carl."

Chapter 7

Dwane smiled a little to himself as they ate in silence for a bit. He hadn't been sure whether or not Laura would appreciate a hot sausage sandwich, but he was very pleased since, while she wasn't quite devouring it, she was definitely eating it with more gusto than she showed her peanut butter and jelly.

He had said she was slender; he had left out the fact that she was "too" slender. Not that he was trying to put meat on her bones or anything, because he was barely an acquaintance, probably not a friend.

Definitely not someone who should be trying to help her.

Not that he even knew what she needed help with. He just knew that she got tired easily, and he supposed that's probably why she ended up falling down the stairs. She'd just been so tired she hadn't lifted her foot enough and tripped.

But why? And he thought he heard that she was recovering. Recovering from what? Would she ever be better?

They weren't really questions he should care about, normally wouldn't think twice about them, but she prompted that in him. And he wanted to know more.

He was finished with the sandwich and dabbing at his fries, while she wasn't quite half done.

"I think you're enjoying that a little more than your regular lunch."

"You're right. I definitely am. I hadn't even realized I was hungry for hot sausage until you set it in front of me and I started smelling it. My stomach woke up for the first time in forever."

"In forever? It woke up?" He wanted to ask more. She had said that much; surely, he could ask her about it.

But her face shut down, and he thought she wasn't going to tell him anything. She swallowed what she had in her mouth and studied the sandwich in front of her before she said, "In a year. It's probably been a year. For a long time, food didn't even taste good."

Her voice was soft, and he figured she was telling him something that was maybe a little hard for her to share, but then she brightened and smiled, looking up at him. "But this is delicious. It's every bit as amazing as I remember it."

"You know I've not been in Blueberry Beach very long, but I can't imagine leaving it. It really kind of grabs a hold of you. Man, the view of Lake Michigan. It's gorgeous. And the breeze, constant and refreshing... I haven't met a single person that wasn't friendly. Just like Zoriah. Everyone here seems to be close-knit, almost like family."

She nodded, having to agree. "You know, I guess my only excuse is when you're young, you're not very smart sometimes. I thought there were a lot of better things out in the world, but I realized I was wrong.

At least, wrong for me. I just feel like I'm home coming back here."

"I can see why."

"But," she had to be fair, "there aren't a whole lot of jobs. Although now that they put the hospital in, that's doubtlessly created jobs, along with the new stores that have gone up around it—the fast-food restaurants, and they're even putting a big department store in there. That helps, but...it changes things too."

Chapter 8

Dwane was silent for a bit, munching on fries, thinking about what Laura said.

He knew she was right. There really wasn't much opportunity for jobs, although he'd been running around a scenario in his head, just a thought, an idea. It wasn't insulting to say it wasn't something that anyone could do. A man needed some knowledge and a bit of money behind him.

"I guess that's the problem with small towns. They're really great to live in, but in order to be able to stay in a small town, you need to have a job, and then, once you start doing things like adding hos-pitals and stores, it changes things and you don't have your small-town sense of community anymore." He dipped a fry in some ketchup. "I guess you could say it's a no-win situation, but I don't know if that's true either."

"No. Just some people have to leave. Some people could stay. And some people come back and have a place. I'm one of the lucky ones, I guess." She smiled, and he felt that strange little sensation in his chest that he'd been feeling every time this week she had smiled at him.

They hadn't talked much, but there was something about her that drew him, some-thing that he really couldn't put his finger on but that made him want to...cultivate a relationship might be a little strong. But at least be friends. Or good friends. Not just casual friends that happened to work in the same place and talked while they did. He wanted to mean something to her, since she was beginning to mean something to him.

"I have to say, this is the best meal I've had all week."

"Me too."

"You probably get sick of your own cooking as I do, and I'm not even that good at it. Actually, that's really stretching the truth. I'm a terrible cook."

She laughed. "It's something that I've always loved, although..." Her voice trailed off, like she'd been about to say something about her past that maybe she didn't want to share. Every time she did that, it made him more curious as to what she was hiding. Maybe he didn't want to know.

"Although what?" he prompted when she didn't say anything more.

"Although in the past few years, I haven't cooked nearly as much as what I wanted to. That's another nice thing about coming back to Blueberry Beach. There's more time to do those things I love. I just need the energy."

"That's tough."

"It is. But I'm cooking every day anyway, maybe you can come eat with us sometime. It's kinda silly for us to eat downstairs and you eat upstairs alone, cooking separate meals."

He should gracefully decline. Or at least protest, but he didn't do either.

"I suppose it's rude of me to say yes. But yes. I'll come eat with you whenever you want. I already told you I'm a terrible cook, and that is one of the downsides of being a terrible cook and living in a small town. There aren't a lot of places where you can go to get meals, and you're kind of stuck with your own terrible cooking."

"Well, it doesn't really look like you're wasting away to nothing, so I'm not going to feel too bad for you. How about tomorrow night?"

It happened to be Friday, but it wasn't a date. Not with her girls and her grandfather all going to be there.

Still, he did smile a little when he said, "Sounds good. I'll bring dessert. How's that?"

"Are you making it yourself?" she asked skeptically. "After you've just spent the last five minutes telling me what a terrible cook you are, I'm a little afraid to have you bringing food into my house."

"No. I promise. Someone else will make the dessert, and I'll just bring it."

"Then it's a deal."

She wiped her hands on her napkin and then balled her garbage up, standing carefully. "I cannot believe I just ate that entire sandwich. I can't remember the last time I ate that much, but it was delicious. Thank you very much."

"My pleasure. Consider it a little prepayment on the supper that you're gonna cook for me."

"That's a lot of pressure," she said as she walked slowly to the garbage can, grabbing his garbage as she went. "I'm not sure I can handle it."

There was irony in her voice, and he wondered if she worked under a lot of pressure before she moved back to Blueberry Beach.

He wanted to ask "why did you move back," because he felt like there was a lot more to it than realizing she wasn't very smart—her words—and missed the small town.

He also felt there might be a connection there between her being so tired all the time and the reason she moved back. It felt like there was a piece missing that would make everything make sense.

Maybe, if they had supper together, he could get her to take a walk with him, and they could talk about it then. He didn't really want to push her now, not when she was finally loosening up just a little with him.

She sat down without saying anything more and opened up her paints.

"I still have a few more minutes before I have to go back out, although if a customer walks in, I'll take care of them. Do you mind if I look over your shoulder?" He could see the door just fine and would be able to help anyone who walked in.

Her grandfather had said he had an appointment today, but he hadn't said what for. Maybe Laura knew, but he didn't want to ask questions that might disturb her from her work.

"Sure." She gave a little self-conscious laugh. "I think I can work with people looking over my shoulder. I do it with my children all the time, although I have to remind them not to bump me. Is that something I'm going to need to say to you?" she asked with a tilted head as he moved behind her.

"I think I can manage to keep my hands to myself. At least I can promise I won't touch you. So I guess you don't have to worry about me bumping you, either."

She carefully unscrewed the container of paint and took a brush out of the water, dabbing it on the cloth she had and then gently picking up the wooden table piece in front of her and looking it over a little.

"Are you deciding what color you want to use?"

"Maybe. A little. I'm picturing it in my head as I want it to be. Thinking about what that's going to take. I know not everyone sees pictures in their head, but I can look at a piece and see it completely finished with all of the details, and all I have to do is get that out of my head and onto the brush and onto the piece I'm working on."

"You must have quite a collection in your head then."

"I guess. It's just when I see an unfinished piece, I can picture what it should look like when it's done. I suppose that's not so uncommon, but I'm also able to actually make it look that way. Which I think is a little more rare."

"I could draw okay in school. I never really had the opportunity to practice much."

"Grandfather said the couple of times you guys have carved together, he thinks you might have the ability to be a decent one. Has he said that to you?"

"The old man doesn't talk much," Dwane said with a grunt. "But he did say something like, 'maybe you won't destroy this quite as bad as I thought you were going to.'" He chuckled at the taciturn man who apparently didn't want to give him a compliment.

Laura laughed, not a full-on laugh but a softer sound, one that he felt curl around his stomach and squeeze. Not an unpleas-ant feeling. And definitely not an unpleas-ant sound. One he'd like to hear again.

"That sounds like Grandfather. That's the way he talks to people when he's teaching them. I think he thinks if he says too many good things, it will go to their head and ruin them. Whatever ruining them means."

"I think compliments encourage people, not the other way around."

"I agree. I try to do that with my girls. Com-pliment to encourage."

"That's the best kind of childhood to have."

"Not the kind you had?" she asked, and it was said casually, like she didn't even realize she might be prying.

His childhood wasn't terrible, but he hadn't been complimented much. Maybe that's why he worked so hard, trying to "prove" he was successful. It wasn't something he wanted to look into. Thankfully, he was saved by his phone ringing.

"Excuse me," he said, and she nodded, before he backed away and swiped his phone.

"Hello?" he said.

"Is this Dwane Hardy?" a lady's voice said.

"It is. What can I do for you?" he said, wondering if this was someone from the business that he and his friend had who hadn't heard that he'd sold out. It would be odd that they would be calling his personal cell phone but not completely unheard of.

"My name is Dawn Putt, and I've been taking care of your daughter."

The woman might have said more, but Dwane didn't hear it. That first sentence was enough to send his brain into shock.

He didn't have children. None that he knew of. And for the last seven years, there wasn't a chance for him to have any children.

Unfortunately, in the years prior to that, he supposed it was very possible that there was a child he didn't know about.

To his shame.

He hadn't even realized he'd walked to the doorjamb and leaned his head against it. He pulled his mind back and said into the silence of the phone, "Would you please repeat that? I don't think I heard you correctly."

"I'm sorry. I didn't think my daughter had told you about her. She got angry every time I asked her if she did, so I quit years ago."

"Years ago. How long ago? How old is she?"

"My daughter is forty, but she acts like a twelve-year-old."

"My daughter. How old is my daughter?" He felt like his words were coming from someone else from somewhere far away.

"Oh. I'm sorry. Of course. She's ten. And I assume you probably didn't know about her. But I've been raising her, and I've just been diagnosed with pancreatic cancer. My outlook isn't good. As much as I love my own daughter, she has never been a steady influence in her daughter's life. In fact, it's all I can do to get her to be an influence at all. I haven't seen her for three weeks, and it's not uncommon for her to take off for more than that at a time."

"She's ten?" he said, his voice soft. It felt almost dreamy. He had a daughter. A ten-year-old daughter. A little girl. He hadn't even known. That was crazy.

"Yes. She's ten and just completing fifth grade. She's a really well-behaved child for the roughness of her life. I've done what I could to make it smooth and easy for her. But there have been times of heartbreak because she knows her mother doesn't really care about her, doesn't want her."

"Does she know she has a father who does?" he asked, his words coming out much rougher, fiercer, than he meant for them to.

"No. But I'm going to tell her if you do. And I'd like for you... I'd like for you to take her. I've looked you up online, once I got your name out of my daughter, and it looks like you're a successful business-man. If you don't want her," those words were slow, drawn out, like she was hoping she was wrong when she said it, but that it had to be said, "then can you at least hire someone? I hate to send her to boarding school, and I don't want to do this, but I need to know that she's settled before I begin treatments. I've heard they're quite rigorous, and I'm going to be struggling to take care of myself, to pay for myself."

He had money. He could do it. He could easily afford a daughter. He didn't have to work the rest of his life if he didn't want to, and here he was just wondering what in the world he would do. Now he knew.

He had a daughter to raise.

He stood up straight, his fingers clutching the phone.

What did he know about raising daughters? What did he know about raising anything?

He was a businessman and entrepreneur. He could exercise, and he could even be a personal trainer. He could probably even repair exercise equipment if he really needed to, but raise a child? A girl? He had three brothers, that was it. He knew nothing about girls.

"When can I get her?" It sounded like the lady was going to just drop her off with him. Like he didn't even have to pass a parenting test. Was there such a thing? Could just anyone become a parent?

Apparently. But the fact that he even thought there should be a test probably meant he was definitely not qualified. Anyone who didn't even know they were a parent—for a decade—certainly couldn't be qualified to raise a child.

"Any time. The sooner, the better. Although she has another week of school, and it would probably be best to let her finish. My treatments start next week as well, and I would feel so much better if I knew her future was settled."

"It will be. You can stop worrying about that. What day is she done with school?"

"Wednesday, she has a few hours in the morning, then that's it for the year."

"I'll be there on Wednesday." Then he realized he didn't even know where she was. "Where is 'there?'"

For the first time, the lady chuckled. "East of Chicago."

He'd spent some time in Chicago opening up five membership-only gyms eleven years ago.

His daughter was most likely a result of that trip.

Man. He was stupid.

"Would you give me your number? And you can give me your address. I'll be there Wednesday... Lunchtime?"

"Yes. That's fine," the lady said and then rattled off her number. He had the presence of mind to be able to program it into his phone, but that's about all he felt like he could do. This had been such a surprise. Not something he had anticipated, obviously.

"I'll be there," he said as he sent her a simple text so she'd have his number. "You'll send me the address?"

"I will. I will tell her she has a father who wants her."

It was unbelievable that a child could be shuffled around like this. Just give her to anyone.

Immediately, he knew he needed to call his lawyers and get them on this. He didn't want to have her, only to have her mother be able to take her away.

He got a little more information from the lady, putting it into the notes of his phone, before they hung up.

He stood, his head down, staring at his phone, still in complete shock and disbelief that he was a father, had been a father for ten years, and hadn't even known it. So unbelievable, so hard to understand...he felt like such a loser.

He should have been involved in his daughter's life. What had she suffered because he hadn't been there? How could he have made her life better? Surely there were things he could have done. Things he should have done.

Guilt threatened to rise up and overwhelm him, and he took a deep breath.

"So finding out you had a daughter was a shock?" Even though Laura's voice was soft and gentle, it hit him like ice-cold water. He had totally forgotten he was standing in the workshop.

His head jerked up. His face felt heavy, his brows lowered, his mouth unable to smile.

"To say the least."

"If there's anything I can do, let me know. I know I sleep a lot, but when I'm not sleep-ing and working, I'll help you if I can."

"I'll keep that in mind." Their eyes met across the room. Hers, caring. His...he didn't even know what. Hopefully, he was moving past the shock into the acceptance and planning stage where he figured out that the rest of his life was going to be completely different than what he thought it was going to be.

"I better get out to the store. I should do some dusting." He'd spent hours dusting yesterday, and it didn't need it, but he just needed to be alone to think. To absorb this shock. And to make a plan.

Chapter 9

Laura looked at the table one more time.

It looked the way it always did, except it had one extra plate on it.

She put a hand on her stomach and used the other hand to push her hair back away from her face.

Tempted to walk to the mirror to see if it was as wild and crazy as she felt it was, she forced herself not to. This was not a date. This was not even a precursor to a date. This was her inviting the neighbor to come eat with them since he was alone and had to cook for himself all the time.

This was her family doing a good deed. Not her trying to impress anyone.

Her stomach fluttered and twirled under her hand. And the desire to look in a mirror hadn't left.

Maybe her mind knew that this was nothing more than a neighborly thing, but the rest of her really seemed to want to make it into something more. Which scared her. And made her want to cancel everything.

She hadn't made anything fancy, just a chicken casserole along with salad and bread.

"Mommy, is it time to eat yet?" Alessandra said from where she sat at the small side table coloring with her sister, Grace.

"Not quite yet, honey." Laura walked over to the table. Maybe it was her imagination, but she felt better today than she had yesterday. Like getting away from the stressful environment and just doing something she loved—painting the figurines that her grandfather carved—and getting to spend time with her girls, without the cloud of what her husband had done between them, had given her new life. Although the new life was dawning slowly.

"Look at what I drew," Grace said, holding up a paper with a big orange circle and some brown around the edges.

Two brown lines came out of the bottom. Laura had looked at enough of Alessandra's papers when she was that age to recognize that that might possibly be a person.

"Did you draw a picture of me?" she asked her daughter with a smile and a surprised look on her face, putting her hand to her chest like she couldn't believe it.

Grace nodded. Great big nods that took her head from looking at the ceiling to looking at the floor and back again.

Laura smiled, feeling peace settle down into her soul. It didn't matter what Christian did. It didn't matter who he ran off with or what he had taken from her. As long as she had her daughters, she had what was important.

Grandfather had provided a roof over their heads and a job for her, and she had a no-stress evening ahead, except...she was a little stressed. Maybe she was stressed in a good way, because as much as she wanted to deny it, she really did care what Dwane thought.

Not that she ever thought he would see anything in someone who was as broken as she was.

She felt broken, though maybe she didn't look it. But he certainly wouldn't be under any delusions after seeing her fall down the stairs and needing to carry her to the couch.

"See, Mommy? That's your hair."

Alessandra looked at her sister's paper, pressing her lips together, but she didn't say anything.

Laura could almost read her mind, knowing that she would like to tell her sister that that didn't look anything like a person, but maybe she remembered her mother's encouragements, and indeed, her lips loosened, and she pointed at Grace's picture. "You made her hair long and pretty like Mommy's used to be."

That was the last thing she had done before she packed up and moved. Cut her hair into a more modern style.

She'd only been married with children for less than ten years, but it was hard to keep up with looking stylish and chic, not motherly and haphazardly put together, when one had small children at home.

The children had always been her responsibility.

Not that she minded. Especially not now.

"I liked your hair better when it was long, Mommy," Alessandra said seriously.

"It will grow back. That's the thing with hair. Cutting it off isn't the end of the world," she said as she walked around the little table to look at Alessandra's picture.

It broke her heart. It was obviously two little girls, with a mom and a dad in the middle, holding onto each of their hands.

She wanted her family back with a fierceness that sent shock waves down her arms that tingled in her fingers. They curled, and she took a calming breath. That wasn't going to be her life, and it would be best for everyone, and for her health, if she accepted it.

Still, she wanted to make sure that Alessandra got attention for her picture too, so she said, "And what did you draw? Is that you and Grace on the ends?" she asked, hoping Alessandra didn't have a meltdown about wanting her family back.

"Yep. That's me and Grace, and that's you." She pointed to the person on her paper with the long brown strands falling down over rather wide shoulders.

Laura held her breath as Alessandra's finger moved toward the bigger person with short hair. A man.

"And that's your new boyfriend."

Her breath came out in a cough. That was not what she was expecting. She was expecting for Alessandra to say that was Daddy and to make her feel guilty for not being with him.

She most definitely wasn't expecting to be told she had a new boyfriend.

Before she could say anything, Alessandra went on. "The last time we saw Daddy, he told us he was going to introduce us to his new girlfriend. But he never did before he left. And if he can have a new girlfriend, you can have a new boyfriend, right, Mommy?" Her words sounded serious until she got to the last two which seemed insecure, and she bit her lip.

Laura felt like she was reeling. She hadn't realized Christian had told them that he had a girlfriend. "You didn't tell me that Daddy had a girlfriend," she tried to say calmly, like they were talking about whether or not the sky was purple.

She didn't want her children to know things she didn't know they knew. Not about this. If Christian was going to tell them about his girlfriend, she felt like she should have known. Because until he told them, her girls hadn't known at all. She hadn't mentioned the reason she wasn't good enough was because he found some-one better.

She was out of breath suddenly, and her knees felt weak. So much for feeling bet-ter.

"Daddy told us not to tell you. He said it would upset you. But I didn't think it would.

But I didn't tell you because I want to listen to Daddy. Daddy lied. Because he never showed us his girlfriend. So I don't have to do what he said, and I can tell you about it if I want to." Alessandra had started coloring again as she spoke, filling in the edges of her paper with the pretty blue. She kept coloring after she was finished, almost like she needed to keep her little hands busy so her brain didn't get too upset about the complicated things she was discussing.

Things a little girl shouldn't have to worry about.

Things Laura would never have made her little girls worry about, if she could have chosen.

Unfortunately, she hadn't been given a choice.

She grabbed a chair from the dining room, checking the time. Ten minutes before they were supposed to start eating. Grandfather would be in any minute. The store would be locked up already, and he would be sweeping up and making sure everything was ready for tomorrow morning. Turning the signs over, pulling the blinds down, checking out the income for the day, making sure of any orders that needed to be placed or had arrived.

She didn't have much time, but she felt she needed to address this with her daughter. Not for the first time, but that's why children had a long childhood, so she had time to tell them something over and over and over again until they got it.

"Alessandra, just because someone breaks their word to you doesn't make it okay for you to break your word to them. If you promised Daddy that you wouldn't say anything, you need to try to do as you said."

"But he didn't," she said without looking up or stopping her coloring.

"But that doesn't make it right for you to not do something. Right?"

Alessandra lifted her shoulders.

"What about this? If you come in my room and rip up all of my books, does it make it okay for me to go into your room and rip up yours?" Aside from her stuffed animal Annie, Alessandra's books were her most treasured possessions.

"If you do it to me, I can do it back to you, to get you back."

"That's the way we want to think. But if we're going to do right, we can't be unkind to people just because they're unkind to us. In fact, the Bible tells us we're to go even further and be extra nice to people who are unkind to us. Blessing them, doing nice things, and praying for them even when they're mean to us."

Alessandra's lip came out, and, while it was a difficult concept for anyone to grasp, but especially an eight-year-old, Laura knew she was understanding a little at least. And even at the same time she was talking to her daughter, she was thinking about her ex and how he'd been unkind to her, and she had not gone out of her way to do anything nice back to him. She'd been too busy withstanding the blows.

She didn't really have to think about it, because she knew there was no place in the Bible that gave an exception to that command. And it was a command. To bless those that curse you and who despitefully use you.

Funny how God could use her children to show her where she wasn't doing right. How she had the same thought in her head that her child had. She didn't want to be nice to Christian, because he had been so mean to her. She wanted to get him back, not bless him.

Knowing that lesson wasn't going to be learned in one day, she changed the subject a little, even though she knew in her heart that God had instigated this conversation, not necessarily because Alessandra needed it but because she did.

"But I will say that any time someone tells you they're going to tell you something that they don't want you to tell your mom or tell your dad, you should run to your parents right away and tell them. Unless it's a birthday surprise or a Christmas surprise," she added.

Alessandra looked up. "Even if Daddy tells me not to tell you?"

"Yes. There shouldn't be any secrets that you're keeping from your parents. And I promise I will try to never ask you to keep a secret from your dad." She hoped she could keep that promise, because it was the right one. Even if she didn't like him, even if she didn't feel like he had the best interests of her children at heart, that he was selfish and immature, it still wasn't right to keep secrets from a parent.

"What if he asks me to?"

"If someone asks you to do something that you know you shouldn't, it's always okay to say 'I know I shouldn't do that, so I'm not going to' as long as you say it respectfully."

Alessandra's lip came out again as she colored on her paper. "So if Daddy says 'don't tell your mom,' I should say no?"

Laura had taught both of her girls never to tell their parents no, not in a disrespectful way.

"If he says 'I want to tell you something, but I don't want you to tell your mom,' you can say 'Mom said it's not a good idea to keep secrets from your parents.'"

There was always the chance that Christian would navigate around that and force

Alessandra to keep secrets, but she didn't want her daughter to feel guilty. "If he won't listen, that's not your fault, and he's putting you in a really hard place. Let's pray that he doesn't do that."

The whole conversation had made her tired, and she wanted to go lie down rather than get up and be ready to serve a meal, but she wasn't entirely sure that she'd done a good job. She hadn't anticipated parenting by herself. Or parenting with someone who was so far away.

"Look at this, Mommy!" Grace said, holding up a different paper.

This one had four oval type circles, with lines sticking out of the bottoms of them. Laura said, "Did you draw you and Alessandra as well?"

"Yep," Grace said proudly with more big nods of her head. "And this is you and your new boyfriend."

"Is Mr. Dwane your boyfriend?" Alessandra asked, almost as though she was putting together the idea of a boyfriend and the fact that there was a man coming for supper tonight.

"No. Not at all. He's just what I told you. The man who lives upstairs that we haven't met yet."

She drove to school to pick her girls up, and they always came in the back, not through the store, so they hadn't been in the shop when Dwane was there. Tonight would be their first time meeting him.

"Maybe I could ask him if he would be your boyfriend. That way you can have a boyfriend just like Daddy has a girlfriend," Alessandra said, her eyes on her paper, her hand coloring, and her little brain having absolutely no idea the chaos she caused in her mother's chest by her words.

"Let's not talk about boyfriends and girl-friends tonight, okay? That's not what Mr. Dwane is. He's our neighbor. Not a boyfriend." Laura tried to keep the panic out of her voice, although she couldn't still the anxiety in her chest that made her push her chair back and stand.

Another hour, maybe two at the very, very most, and then she'd be able to lie down on the couch while the girls listened to Grandfather play his bagpipes.

Maybe if she had a few minutes to rest, she would get her cello out and play with him.

She hadn't thought to ask Dwane if he played an instrument. But, remembering the athletic shorts, the bulging T-shirt, and the music thumping out of his speakers, she highly doubted it. Not to be judgmental, but he just didn't seem like the instrument-playing type.

Maybe she was jumping to conclusions.

Again, she felt it was doubtful.

"Okay, girls, let's get these crayons and papers picked up. I'm going to need you to help me finish carrying the stuff out to the table."

"I'm hungry," Grace said to no one in particular as she immediately started putting her crayons away. Nothing like hunger to induce a child to be obedient.

"That's good. We have a big supper planned, and I know it's going to be delicious because I had the best helpers in the world helping me make it. I can't wait to try it."

"Me either," Alessandra said. "I can't wait to go to school Monday and tell everybody I helped make dinner for our guest."

Laura smiled at her daughter as the sound of the back door opening reached them, and she ran her hands down her jeans.

There was no reason to be nervous. She wasn't trying to impress anyone. She was just trying to be hospitable.

Chapter 10

Dwane shifted the two tubs of ice cream in his hand and knocked on the door.

Gavin had allowed him to leave ten minutes early in order to go to the store and purchase it.

It was now half past, and he was right on time.

If there was anything he had learned from his years of owning his own business, it was that a person needed to be on time if he expected anyone else to be.

He supposed the habit was so ingrained he hadn't even thought about it, just kept an eye on the clock and did what he could, judging the time and making sure it wasn't getting away from him.

He wasn't trying to impress anyone.

Even as he thought that to himself, he knew it wasn't really true. Laura, despite seeming like his opposite, intrigued him in a way that no one ever had.

Certainly, she was the first woman to catch his eye since he got serious about living his life for the Lord.

Maybe she was just a distraction, something that would pull him away from whatever it was he was supposed to be doing here in Blueberry Beach.

Or maybe she was the reason he was here in Blueberry Beach.

He had left her kind of abruptly yesterday when he found out about his daughter. Now, he'd had twenty-four hours to get used to it, and although he hadn't quite figured things out, he was much more confident and the shock had faded.

It had been unexpected, to say the very least, but he was happy about it for the most part. He wanted to get to know his girl. Wanted to have a part in her life. Wanted to be there to raise her. To give her advice, to teach her, to do all those things a father was supposed to do.

His own father had been a great dad for the most part, and Dwane had a great example. Unfortunately, Blueberry

Beach, Michigan, was awfully far away from Phoenix where his dad and mother had retired.

He was eager to pick her up, couldn't wait for next Wednesday in fact.

The only problem he had was when he'd texted Dawn back, she'd suggested he bring his mother with him since his daughter was apparently not familiar with men and typically didn't warm up to them very quickly.

That was a rather large problem since his mother was in Phoenix, and he hadn't even told his parents he had a child.

The door opened, bringing his thoughts back to the present. The cramping in his stomach reminded him that for some odd reason he was nervous.

"Mommy said I could answer the door," the little girl said, blinking up at him with big brown eyes. They contrasted with her long blonde hair and pale skin. She had a huge smile on her face, and she looked pretty proud of herself.

"Oh, she did?" he said, returning the little girl's grin. "That's probably because you do such a good job opening the door."

He hadn't been around many children. His younger brothers hadn't gotten married yet, either.

"I never got to do it before when we had company," the little girl said conversationally. "But I practiced before you came, and I did okay."

"Practicing is good. I think that's wise." He shifted the ice cream into his left hand

and held out his right. "I'm Dwane, and I'm happy to meet you."

The little girl looked at his hand like she'd never seen an adult hand before.

A shadow fell on her shoulder, but Dwane didn't look up.

"That's where you say, 'I'm Alessandra, and I'm happy to meet you.' Then you shake his hand," Laura said in a soft voice like she was just talking to her daughter and Dwane couldn't hear.

"I'm happy meeting you," Alessandra said dutifully as she grabbed a hold of his large hand in her left hand and tilted her head like she couldn't quite understand why the shaking wasn't working very well while she pumped his hand up and down.

"Use your other hand, sweetheart," Laura said softly again to her little girl.

"This one?" Alessandra asked, holding up her right hand.

He lifted his eyes just in time to see Laura's eyes flash with humor. If it were his little girl, he might say something like, "no, your other other hand."

Regardless, he had to smile, just because Alessandra was so cute.

"Yes, sweetie."

Alessandra pulled her left hand out and grabbed his hand with her right, pumping just as hard as before.

Laura smiled again, and he loved the way her face came alive when it was lit up by a grin. With her wavy brown hair that framed her face and her brown eyes that looked so much like her daughter's, she was beautiful in a way that was real and genuine and that tugged at his heart.

"I'm pleased to meet you, Alessandra," he said in his best gentleman's voice.

"Me too," she said, abruptly dropping his hand. "Mom said you can come in, although I told Grace I wouldn't let you in if you didn't have dessert. Because Mom didn't make any."

She looked up at him and put a little hand on her hip, jutting it out.

"Alessandra! That is not kind," Laura said, sounding shocked that her child would say such a thing. Although in his—very limited—experience with children, you just never knew what was going to come out of their mouth.

"I think it's nice that you made a pact with your sister. Sometimes, sisters don't get along. I'm glad that you do."

"We don't get along most of the time, but we both like dessert. So I agreed with her when she said that we shouldn't let you in if you don't have it." She narrowed her eyes at the bag in his left hand. "Is that dessert?"

"Maybe," he said cagily. "What's on the menu tonight? If it's not any good, maybe I'll just go to my apartment and eat this ice cream myself."

"It's chicken casserole, and I helped make it, so it's going to be good." Her little voice had all the confidence in the world. What a precocious child.

"That so? So your mom is not a good cook?"

"Mommy is the best cook in the world. But I'm her best helper." Her lips pulled back just a little bit like she was forcing herself to say the next words. "Along with Grace. Although Grace is a baby and not able to do all the things I can do. Mommy even let me cut the chicken up with the knife as long as I was careful."

"How many fingers did you cut off?"

"None," she said like it was a ridiculous question, although she giggled a little too like she found him funny.

"You'd better hold your hands up so I can check. I'm not sure I want to come up if I'm going to find a finger in my chicken casserole."

She held all of her fingers up, flipping her hands back and forth, before she said, "Now you hold your hands up. I don't want you to come in with ice cream if there's fingers in it."

"I just bought it at the ice cream shop. I wasn't cutting anything up and putting it in the container."

"I need to see your hands anyway."

"Alessandra!" Laura said, still sounding shocked.

Dwane grinned at her to let her know it was okay before he held up the hand that wasn't holding the bag of ice cream.

Then he scrunched his hands together behind the bag. "Hang on a second." He turned his back a little. "I have to flip this fake finger from one hand to the other, because I only have one fake finger and I chopped two off."

"There," he said, turning back around and holding up the hand that had been holding the bag before. "All five."

Alessandra had her arms crossed over her chest and her eyes narrowed like she wasn't quite sure whether he was serious or not.

"Let me see your other hand," she said suspiciously.

"I already showed it to you."

"I want to see them both at the same time."

"But I'm holding the bag. I can't hold both up."

"I just need to make sure there's no fingers in the ice cream. And then you can come in."

"Tell you what, I'm going to take your mom, she and I will go to my apartment, and your mom and I are going to get spoons, and we'll each get a carton of ice cream to ourselves. You can have the chicken casserole. How's that?"

She stood and looked at him for a couple of moments, rolling over what he'd said in her mind. Just to force her hand, he looked at Laura, who had her mouth open and seemed like she wasn't quite quick enough to keep up with their conversation or wasn't used to someone teasing her girls—although he got the impression she liked it—and didn't know whether to yell at him or her daughter.

He held his hand out. "Ms. Laura? Will you eat ice cream with me upstairs?"

That did it.

"You can come in," Alessandra said. "But I want to see your hands as soon as you set the ice cream down."

"Alessandra, that is quite enough. He doesn't have any fingers in the ice cream, even if he is missing one or two," Laura said, and he heard the humor in her voice. He loved that she was laughing at him and not annoyed that he was teasing her daughter.

"Grace is gonna show you where you can put the ice cream, and then we're gonna show you where you can sit down," Alessandra said as she turned to walk into the room.

He stepped in, closing the door behind him.

Laura was still standing there, and he found himself not wanting to move away from her.

She leaned into him a little bit. "Thank you. It's funny how men and women are different, and I never think to tease her like that. It's good for her."

"I guess that's why God gave kids a mom and dad. We treat kids differently, and they need both."

"I agree. Thank you."

He wanted to ask where Alessandra's dad was, but he assumed he must be absent if Laura was thanking him for acting like a man with her daughter. Still, curiosity was there, stronger.

She was close enough that he was able to catch her scent of smiles and sunshine and something that felt like home.

He wanted to breathe deeply, move closer, but she seemed to be waiting for him to follow Alessandra, so he did, stepping fully into the house, looking around.

He said over his shoulder, "The last time I was in here, I didn't look around too much. I was more concerned about you."

He waited for her to catch up to him so they could walk side by side. She didn't seem put off that he had reminded her of what happened when they first met. And he was happy about that. He wasn't sure exactly what the problem was, but he didn't want her to feel like she had to hide it from him.

"There's not much to look at. It's pretty small. Probably there are too many of us living here right now, but Grandfather has been good."

He opened his mouth to say something more, but Gavin walked in, and he turned his eyes to the older man. "Thanks for letting me come over for supper tonight. I told Laura that I'm a terrible cook. She took pity on me. I hope it's okay that she invited me."

"Our doors are always open. Anyone who wants can sidle up to the table, and we'll divide whatever we have equally among us," Gavin said with a grandfatherly grin.

Dwane had the feeling that he actually meant that, and he loved what that said about Gavin and about Laura too, since she had invited him knowing he would be welcome.

He could count on one hand the number of times he'd been invited to eat at someone's house just for an everyday meal and not celebrating something special.

Of course, he didn't need any fingers at all to count the number of times that he'd invited someone to his house for a meal that wasn't a special occasion.

He could hardly complain about other people not doing what he never did.

He'd have to consider that more later. Interesting the little ways a person could grow if they allowed themselves to be open to the idea of change.

A glance over at Laura showed she was helping her youngest place the butter on the table. He had a feeling if he spent much time around that woman, she would be the kind of person who prompted him to be better.

That was the kind of person that he wanted to spend time with.

Chapter 11

"That was perfect, Grace," Laura said as Grace set the butter on the table. "Hop in your seat, and I'll bring the casserole in." Her butterflies were nearly gone after watching Dwane interact with Alessandra at the front door. He had been so good with her, even though he'd been a little awkward and she was pretty sure he wasn't used to being around small children.

Her butterflies might be gone, but that feeling of attraction, that he was different than all the other men she knew, that there was something about him that made her want to know more, had gotten stronger.

Not the kind of feeling she wanted to deal with.

"Go ahead and sit down, Grandfather. I'll bring your water in." Laura turned to Dwane, who had stopped beside the table. "Is water okay? We also have sweet tea if you'd like."

"Water's fine."

She pointed to a chair at the foot of the table. No one ever sat there, since she sat on one side with Grace. Alessandra sat on the other, and Grandfather sat at the head. "You can sit there. I need to carry a couple more things in, and then we're ready."

She walked to the kitchen, grateful to have a couple of moments to compose herself and take a few deep breaths.

"What can I carry in?" Dwane's voice said from behind her, and she managed to hide the fact that it startled her.

"You're the guest. You're not supposed to be working."

"I'm here. Put me to work."

She picked up the hot pads and turned and handed them to him. "There's a hot plate on the table. You can take the casserole and set it on there. I'll get the drinks, and that's it."

"I'll be back in for a couple of drinks then, since I'm sure you can't carry five at once."

"You're right." She laughed a little. "Thanks. I don't think we usually invite people over and then put them to work immediately."

"You can put me to work since I came in here and volunteered." He walked by her carrying the casserole, and she caught a whiff of his scent, honest and true and appealing.

She put ice in the adult glasses and had two plastic cups for her girls, which she filled with ice as well. Dwane was back before she had finished filling the fifth glass with water from the tap, and he picked up the three adult glasses.

"There are those two and anything else?"

"That should be it," she said, shutting the tap off and picking up the girls' glasses.

It was an odd feeling to have someone helping her in the kitchen. Christian certainly never had. Of course, she didn't cook too much when Christian was around. They'd eaten out a good bit and had had a nanny for their children, since she had worked in the office.

Not for the first time, she thought that maybe having Christian leave had been a blessing in disguise. A painful blessing, but one that had brought her closer to her children, because there hadn't been too many times during her marriage with Christian where she'd spent time in the kitchen with her girls or had been relaxed and focused on them enough to show them how to properly set a table or how to clean up afterwards.

All the things she should have been teaching her children had been set aside while she focused on her career and their business.

Dwane stood behind the chair that she planned to sit on, the one beside Grace.

She thought maybe he had misunderstood about where she wanted him to sit and supposed it wouldn't be that big of a deal for her to sit where she'd expected him to, except it might intimidate Grace a little to sit beside a complete stranger. And then she realized he was waiting for her so he could hold her chair for her and help her slide it in.

Something no one had ever done for her, at any time in her life.

She swallowed, because it could end up being awkward, since she had no idea how to do this. Surely it couldn't be that hard to just sit down on the chair and have him slide it in.

Her worry was for nothing as it seemed to go fairly well—she didn't fall to the ground or knock the table over.

She murmured a thank you as he walked around the table to his seat. They all bowed their heads while Grandfather said grace.

Laura kept her hands folded in her lap, saying a private prayer of her own, thanking the Lord that she actually felt better today. The heaviness wasn't quite so bad, the feeling that her limbs were deadweight was almost gone.

Maybe the doctors had been right. She had certainly been skeptical when they'd said it was all due to stress, but coming to Blueberry Beach and determining to shed the anxiety of not having her husband around, and wondering what he was doing, and who he was with, and wondering why God would bless him when he'd been so terrible to her, just getting rid of all of that had made her future seem brighter. And her burdens in life seem lighter.

Maybe she would climb out of this pit after all.

"Amen," her grandfather said, and she murmured a soft amen with her girls, joined by the deeper amen of Dwane.

There wasn't much conversation as they passed the food around, with Laura serving Grace but allowing Alessandra to serve herself, reminding her to eat what she took.

The chicken casserole was something that both of her girls loved, which was part of the reason she was serving it.

While they were good eaters, she didn't want any chance of a meltdown with Dwane at the table. Not that she was trying to impress him, and not that her girls typically had meltdowns, but in her experience as a parent, they happened when you least expected them.

"So, I've noticed the empty building beside our store, and I was wondering what used to be there," Dwane said after the food had been passed and they had started eating.

"Used to be a train shop," her grandfather said immediately, bringing a smile to Laura's face. She remembered spending many happy hours of her childhood watching the trains in that shop go around. "When Ray died, none of his kids wanted to have anything to do with it, and they sold what was left and shuttered the shop."

"I see," Dwane said and then added, "That's too bad. Sounds like a fun shop. One I would enjoy anyway."

"Oh, it was fun," Laura said. "I spent a lot of hours watching the trains. He had some interactive displays that were set up permanently, not for sale of course, where you could start and stop them or make trucks go back and forth or something. It was a really neat place to be. Magical. Like stores aren't anymore."

She looked at her daughters, wishing they could have had the experience that she did. Loving how those memories took her back to her childhood, even just talking about them.

"So the building's empty now?" Dwane said.

Her grandfather nodded. "Yeah, they cleaned most everything out. I think a few years ago, it finally went up for tax sale. No one bought it, and now the county owns it, I think. Or whatever happens with that stuff."

"I probably have to go to the county courthouse and find out?" Dwane said, and Laura finally realized he was asking because he was interested in it as a shop for himself.

The idea that he wasn't going to be in their shop forever surprised her. It had barely been a week, and already she kind of just thought that he was a permanent fixture in their store. She should have known better. Their hired help had come and gone so often over the years; she couldn't even remember all of their names.

"I'm sure the records are down there, but Bill probably would know. He gets out a lot more than I do, and he's got his hand in everything."

"Bill?" Dwane asked.

Her grandfather had just put a bite of casserole in his mouth, so Laura said, "He owns the surf shop down the sidewalk from us. He's typically there from ten until six or so, although he was helping out at the diner for a while. I don't think he's do-ing that anymore."

"But he still has Adam working for him. Adam used to own a business back in Pennsylvania, but he sold it and moved out here with his wife and daughter a while back."

"I see. So maybe he's interested in the empty building beside you?" Dwane said.

"I don't think so. His wife owns the can-dy and ice-cream shop. And I don't think they're looking to add anything more to that. Although I could be wrong."

Laura hadn't had a chance to ask her grandfather how his doctor's appointment went, but something in the droop of his eye or maybe in the tone of his voice—it wasn't quite as gruff as it usually was—made her think of it just now.

She made a note to ask him later. He might not even tell her. Sometimes, he didn't talk a lot.

"Are you thinking of putting something in there?" her grandfather said after a minute.

That caught her attention, and Laura listened as she helped Grace put a little more dressing on her salad.

"Maybe. Someone pointed out that Blueberry Beach doesn't have a gym, and it seems like a rather large lack. I was just kind of tossing around the idea in my head but hadn't gotten any further than that."

"Have you owned a business before?" her grandfather asked.

"I have. I sold it before I moved here." Dwane didn't say any more, and Laura wondered exactly what kind of business it was he'd had. Although she couldn't get out of her head that he had said the Lord had moved him to Blueberry Beach and he wasn't sure why. Maybe he thought he'd found out the reason.

"You've been doing good on the carving that we've had the chance to do. Kind of thought you might be thinking about staying for a while and possibly being trained."

She couldn't remember too many times in her life where Grandfather had sounded disappointed. This was one of them.

She didn't think she was the only one who thought maybe Dwane was staying in their shop forever.

"I can't deny, I like it. And I feel like I have a little knack for it, which, if nurtured, might grow into something like a skill."

"That's how I was thinking."

"But I guess my mind is always running on things, and seeing that empty building and knowing that there is a need had me thinking along business lines as well."

"So you're saying you might stay or you might leave?"

"I want to stay, if you'll have me. As long as we're all enjoying the work and things are working out for everyone. But I might do this business thing on the side."

He might be staying after all. Laura didn't know why she was so relieved about that. She hadn't even made a decision about how long she was going to stay.

"I'll have to—"

Her sentence was interrupted by Grace reaching for her drink but somehow knocking it over. Ice water spread diagonally across the table and directly toward Dwane. He jumped up, pushing his chair back, but from the wet stain on his pants, it was obvious he wasn't quite fast enough.

Laura jumped up immediately as well and said, "I'm so sorry," as she hurried into the kitchen to grab a couple of dish towels.

Dwane had his hand on the edge of the table, keeping the water pooling there. She put a towel down to sop up the mess.

While she was doing that, he grabbed the other one and bent over, dabbing up the water that had fallen on the floor.

"You don't have to do that. Honest. Normally, we make our guests stay for at least an hour before we start cracking the whip behind them," she said, trying to lighten the atmosphere a little.

"I guess when you own your own business, you just jump in and do things wherever there is a need. You don't wait for someone to ask you or think it's not your job because it's not in your job description. You just do what needs to be done."

Laura's hand stilled as she dabbed at the water on the table.

That's exactly the way things were in Grandfather's shop. Whatever needed to be done. Helping the customers, carving, painting, cleaning up, making deliveries, or shipping orders, whatever. It was a small shop, and people just pitched in.

She hadn't really thought about this being something unique to people who own their own business, but she supposed it was true, and she had picked it up from her grandfather.

"I'm sorry, Mommy," Grace said from beside her.

Laura looked up, surprised at the tone. She hadn't even thought that Grace might be upset. They spilled things all the time, and it was just a matter of cleaning it up and sitting back down.

Having a guest must have upset her a little more or embarrassed her.

She pressed the towel on the table and scooted around the corner, putting her hand on Grace's back and pulling her to her side.

"It's okay. It's not a big deal. We just clean up and move on. There's nothing harmed."

All things they'd said before. Spilling something at the table wasn't such a big deal.

Her fear that her daughter was going to burst into tears wasn't realized, as Dwane said, "I was a little warm anyway. I'm thankful for you being so considerate and tossing a little of your ice water on me so I could cool down some."

Grace giggled against Laura's side before she said, "It's not that hot out."

"Sometimes, it doesn't have to be hot out for me to be hot."

Laura knew exactly what he was talking about even if he was saying it to be goofy. She'd been nervous and a little anxious about the dinner, and she was kind of warm herself. Not warm enough that she wanted someone to spill their water on her, but warmer than the temperature outside would seem to indicate.

"Next time you get hot, just let Grace know. I'm sure she would be happy to dump even more water on you. Or maybe you could have a water balloon fight. Let's do that outside, okay?"

"A water balloon fight? Could we really?"

"It's supposed to be really warm next week. Maybe we can do it then. Maybe to celebrate school being out."

That brought on a whole new set of worries, since she hadn't heard back from Zoriah about whether or not Macy would be able to watch the girls this summer. She was getting down to the wire, and she really needed to get something figured out.

"Here. I'll take these back out to the kitchen, and hopefully you can sit back down and enjoy the rest of your meal in relative dryness."

Laura picked her towel off the table and held her hand out for Dwane's. Their eyes met as he handed it to her, and his fingers brushed hers, sending a little jolt of electricity up her arm.

It was unexpected and most certainly un-welcome. She decided to ignore it.

Turning, she walked quickly to the kitchen and set the dish towels down.

When she came back, the conversation stayed on neutral topics like the weather, and Dwane didn't mention the building or a business again.

She had wondered if maybe he was thinking about a business because he had found out he was a father and needed to do more than just hang out in Blueberry Beach. But that didn't seem like an appropriate question to ask while her children were sitting there, and her grandfather too. If Dwane had mentioned his impending fatherhood to Grandfather or anyone else, she didn't know about it.

They weren't going to find out from her. That was his news to tell whenever he chose to do so.

Regardless, it didn't matter. She was going to survive this meal and not worry about her handsome neighbor, or the wonderful way he was with her girls, or the tingles that he shot up her arm.

She definitely didn't need that kind of complication in her life.

Chapter 12

Dwane couldn't remember the last time he had a nicer evening. The girls were cute, although not perfect of course, and the family atmosphere settled down around like that pleasantly exhausted feeling after a really great workout.

Gavin had been interesting to talk to, full of stories about Blueberry Beach back in its heyday according to him, and Dwane supposed if he'd have pressed, he could have heard some stories about Laura back in her childhood as well.

Hopefully some other time. Because Laura was the other reason, probably the main one, he considered the evening so nice.

He didn't mean for their eyes to meet so much, but they had, and he felt like there was a conversation flowing between them, independent of the one that was actually happening at the table.

Maybe he wasn't reading her as well as he thought, but he felt like she could read his thoughts, too. It was great to sit with someone who seemed to understand him, even though she didn't really know him that well.

He wanted to change that.

Dwane washed the last ice-cream dish and handed it to Alessandra to dry as Grace and Laura finished wiping the table and put everything away. Grandfather continued to sit at the table with a cup of coffee in front of him.

As he let the water out of the sink, Dwane spoke low to Laura, "It's a nice evening out. Would you like to take a walk?"

Some fleeting expression crossed over her face. He wanted to believe it was an expression of wanting to, because her words were the opposite. "I can't. The girls have school tomorrow, and it's track and field day. I need to make sure that they have everything that they need for that, and..." She gave an apologetic look. "I'm tired."

He nodded, wanting to say that sometimes a walk actually helped with tiredness, but he didn't. He wasn't sure exactly what her issue was, and he wasn't a doctor or anything close, so he didn't want to be pushing her to do something that she shouldn't be doing, especially when he didn't know anything about her.

Still, disappointment threatened to over-whelm all the good feelings that he had had from the evening, and he shrugged it off. "Then I'm going to get going after I thank you, yet again, for the delicious sup-per and for the invitation in the first place. I appreciate it."

"Anytime. Really. The girls are here, and we always have to eat, and you're cer-tainly welcome to eat with us." Something twitched on her face, and he kind of got the impression that she might have been remembering that he would have a daugh-ter soon, too.

He would have his own little family. Him and his daughter. Not much of a family. But it was what he had been given.

He paused, tempted to ask Laura to go with him to pick his daughter up, but he had prayed and told the Lord that if she ended up on the beach with him, he'd ask her. He hadn't been entirely sure that he should take an almost stranger with him, so it felt like that would be the Lord's answer; if they ended up on the beach together, he'd at least ask.

He supposed he shouldn't feel as disappointed as he did about that either, but he wasn't sure what he was going to do if his daughter didn't like him. Who would have thought he could even be worried about such a thing? But he was, for sure.

She'd just have to learn to like him.

He wasn't worried about him liking her. He didn't even know what she looked like or what she enjoyed or any of her experiences so far in life other than she had an absentee mother and a grandmother in failing health and a father she just found out about. Still, he loved her.

"You can stay a while. Go ahead and sit down. You don't need to rush off."

Dwane turned toward Gavin and shook his head. "I've already been here an hour and a half, even though it doesn't feel like it. And I don't want to keep you guys all evening. I do want to get another invitation at some point, and if I overstay my welcome, it might not be forthcoming."

Both Laura and her grandfather laughed at that, and he figured that they really wouldn't mind if he did stay. But he was serious. He didn't want to overstay his welcome. Plus, he needed to get out and think a little.

His daughter was coming, and he was meeting her for the first time. This was not a time to develop a romance anyway. It was a good thing Laura had turned him down. It'd been a bad idea to ask.

He said goodbye to each of the girls, waved at Laura again who smiled at him. He didn't think it was his imagination that she looked a little sad, but he pushed the thought aside and slipped out their apartment door.

His belly was too full for him to take a jog, although it was a perfect evening for one. Not too hot.

But a walk would be nice. So, he slipped out, heading around the building and down the sidewalk to the beach, walking out along Lake Michigan on the sand.

She was gray with just touches of blue tonight, looking like she might be slightly stormy, maybe frowning. Ever-changing, and he loved it. As much as he loved the breeze that blew in almost constantly from the water. Fresh and pure, filling his lungs with all the good things, he could hardly take enough deep breaths to enjoy it as deeply as it deserved.

It was not quite dark when he got back to Main Street. The moon, at three quarters, shone a good bit of light over everything. Enough for him to see the surf shop sign and read it easily. Beneath the sign, a man sat in a camp chair, slouched back, just sitting there watching the empty street like he didn't have anything better to do with his time.

Maybe that was the Bill Gavin had been talking about. Dwane adjusted his direction so he hit the other side of the street and walked up it.

He slowed as he got to the man and said, "Nice evening."

"Sure is. We have a lot of them around here."

"I hope I get to find that out for myself."

"You move into town?"

"Yes, sir. Couple weeks ago. I'm Dwane." He held out his hand.

"Bill. I own this." Bill jerked his head back toward the shop behind him.

"I thought it might be you. I was just talking to Gavin and Laura about you tonight."

"Maybe I don't want to know what about."

"Gavin just said that you might know what was going on with that empty store on the other side of The Little People Shop."

Bill snapped his fingers. "That's where you're from. You're working there now."

"I am." He didn't elaborate. He didn't want to go into the fact that he had moved to Blueberry Beach just because he felt the Lord was telling him to and not because he actually had anything lined up for him to do. He was a little old to be sweeping shavings in a store for a living.

The downward trajectory of his career path might be upsetting to some people, but one of the lessons that had been hammered in his head over and over again was that appearances could be deceiving. Sweeping shavings maybe took a little humility, but there was nothing wrong with that.

"What you want to know about?" Bill asked, jerking his head at the empty store.

"Gavin said that it might have been sold at auction or else the county took it over. He said he figured you'd know."

They talked for a bit while Bill explained to him what happened to the store, and he asked questions, finding out where he would need to go to figure out how to purchase it or if it was even for sale.

If the Lord wanted him to open up a gym in Blueberry Beach, God was going to have to open up the doors to make it happen. So Dwane wasn't too concerned about all the legalities, and he definitely didn't worry about whether or not it was going to work out. If it did, maybe that was the reason why he was here. And if it didn't, obviously it wasn't meant to be. He wasn't going to get his heart set on anything though.

There was no quicker way to disappointment than to get all of his expectations hung on one thing. He'd done that before, and it was a painful landing.

Finally, Bill said, "I hope it works out for you. Blueberry Beach could use a gym.

You'd have my membership. Is that the kind you're going to have?"

"Probably," Dwane said, knowing he wasn't committing to anything.

"Ever own your own business before?" Bill asked, maybe the question of a business owner about to give some advice.

"I did." He wasn't going to get into it, then he figured Bill and he were going to be neighbors, so why not. "I had a buddy that I partnered with, and we ended up with a corporation that owned chains of exercise gyms in Chicago and through the Midwest. It's pretty successful, but he wanted to go in a direction I didn't, and instead of fighting about it, he offered to buy me out. I sold."

"Wishing now you wouldn't have?"

"I don't know. Sometimes I miss it. Sometimes I'm sure that this is the direction I need to go in my life, and I'm glad I did. I can't wait to see what's over the next hill."

"For some of us, it's more of the same. For you, I'm betting not."

"I don't think so. I don't think I'd do it again unless I do it myself. My buddy and I are still friends, and we always will be, but I do think it's much nicer to be able to make decisions on my own, even though I think we complement each other most of the time."

"Like a good marriage."

"I guess."

"Never been?"

"No." He sighed, figuring that he needed to explain, since next week he was going to be walking around with a daughter. "Although I do have a daughter. She'll be living with me starting next Wednesday when I'm going to pick her up."

"I see. Is she about the age of Laura's daughters? They'll have fun playing together this summer."

And just like that, he realized he had no idea what he was going to do with her all summer. His daughter. All summer. He hadn't even given it consideration. He had to work. What was she going to do?

"How old does a kid have to be before you can leave them home by themselves? Especially if home is just upstairs from where you're working?" he asked before he thought about it.

Bill scratched his balding head, then flexed his jaw. "You're asking the wrong person. I don't know much about that kind of thing, but I would say at least, what, ten? Maybe twelve? If you're right there, just down-stairs, probably a little on the younger side."

Maybe he would be able to leave her alone after all. He hardly wanted to, though. Not after he just got her. He supposed it prob-ably depended on the girl too. She might not want to be alone; she might not be trustworthy enough to be left alone. There were too many variables he didn't know. He couldn't make that decision right now.

"Well, thanks a lot for telling me about the old train shop and what happened to it. Sounds like Blueberry Beach really lost something when they lost that."

"They did. It probably wouldn't be profitable now anyway. Toy trains aren't really a thing anymore. Although sometimes, vacationers don't always buy practical things. There's no accounting for their taste."

Dwane laughed. "Has the surf shop been yours all your life?" he asked just to make conversation because he hated to grab the information he needed and run with it.

"I grew up here. Never wanted to leave."

"It's the kind of town that really grabs a hold of you and doesn't want to let go."

"I guess it wasn't just the town. But some things you just can't hold onto," Bill said, which made Dwane wonder about his backstory. There didn't seem to be an easy way to ask, and Bill was looking down at his hands like he didn't want to talk about it anyway.

"You should be looking for an apprentice or something. Someone to take over the surf shop after you're done. You don't want it to meet the same fate as the train shop."

"I guess I should. You never know what's going to happen." Bill paused for a moment and lowered his voice a little. "I heard Gavin had a doctor's appointment today. I suppose I'll find out tomorrow how it went."

"Yeah. I can't help you out there. I knew he had an appointment, and I knew it was at the doctor's, but I guess I was just assuming it was a general checkup."

"I think it might have been slightly more involved than that, but I'm not sure he wants Laura to know."

"That serious?" Dwane said, all his attention focused on Bill. He hadn't even thought that Gavin might be seriously sick. A sore hip, an annual checkup, bloodwork, even high blood pressure or cholesterol or something. He hadn't considered that it might be something more than that.

"That's what he was going today to find out. I haven't heard. But with Laura being back... She's been through quite a lot. I don't think she's ready for another blow like that." Bill looked up at Dwane, almost as though he was taking his measure.

Dwane wasn't sure what kind of measure there was to take, but he hoped he passed muster.

"She could use someone to look after her. Although I'm sure she probably wouldn't appreciate me saying that. She was actually a rather successful businesswoman with her husband, and right now, she's just a shell of her former self. I believe she's recovering. Blueberry Beach is a good place to do that."

"I agree. If you need to relax and recover, this is the place to be. What has she gone through?" Dwane asked, knowing he shouldn't. If he wanted to know, he should go straight to the source. This felt a little bit too much like gossip, but he was curious.

"I guess I probably already said too much. If you're working in the shop with her, she'll talk to you about it eventually. It's not really my place, and I shouldn't have said anything. I'm sorry."

"Not your fault. Don't worry about it. I appreciate you protecting her privacy. If I want to know, I'll ask her."

They chatted about the weather, the tourist season coming out, and the kids getting out of school before Dwane left, walking slowly through the alley to the back side of his apartment.

The place might be relaxing and restful, but it seemed like everyone around had secrets. The person he was most interest-

ed in worked beside him every day. He
needed to ask. Maybe there was something he could do.

Chapter 13

S unday, the shop didn't open until noon, and normally, Grandfather took care of it while she spent the afternoon after church with her daughters.

Monday, the shop was closed, the girls were in school, and she had off.

Which was why, after she had taken the girls to school, she decided to change her shoes and take a walk on the beach.

She hadn't done it since she'd come, since it'd taken all of her energy pretty much to just live.

The change had been gradual, but she realized she was feeling better.

Just getting away from the stress and into a new environment had really helped. Just like the doctors had said, although she hadn't really believed them at the time. She wanted there to be something wrong with her. Something that was fixable, something concrete and absolute. Something she could take a pill for and have it go away. Not this vague, "it's stress and you just need to rest" diagnosis.

With the hope that she might actually start feeling better, maybe get all of her old energy back, and be able to do more than just sludge through each day, she was lost in thought at the opportunities that were suddenly opened in front of her. She didn't realize Dwane was standing in the stairwell, putting his running shoes on, until she had gone out the back door and it was closing behind her.

"Oh!" she said, coming to a complete stop. "I didn't realize you were there."

"Not for long. Just need to finish tying the shoe, and then I'm off for a jog."

At that point, she was tempted to completely scratch her plans to walk along the shore. But it'd been so long since she felt like doing it, and she'd looked forward to it since she'd woken up and actually had some energy, so she didn't. "Maybe we'll see each other. I decided I was going for a walk today too."

She couldn't read his look as he nodded. "Maybe we will."

He jerked his head at her as he straightened, brushing by her with his scent, familiar and very good, lingering as he disappeared.

She could probably drag her feet, and he would be finished, and there wouldn't be any chance of them meeting on the beach.

Of course, there was only a fifty percent chance that they would since she could end up going the exact opposite direction that he did.

Why it was so imperative that she avoid him, she wasn't quite sure. Although she definitely didn't want him to think that she was chasing him around. Because that was most certainly not the case.

Deciding today was a good day to pop in at the diner and pick up the herbal supplements that Iva May had offered her a week ago when she'd come to visit in The Little People Shop, Laura figured if she spent enough time, she might miss Dwane altogether.

With that thought in mind, she had the realization that the heaviness that she'd fought for so long in her limbs and her chest was completely gone. It was probably wishful thinking to think that it was permanently gone.

The idea that there was an end was certainly encouraging. That she would have times of not feeling completely exhausted gave her hope.

She crossed the street to the diner and walked in. It was busy, and she should have known better. The breakfast rush was in full swing.

Still, Iva May stood behind the cash register, checking someone out. She smiled and waved. "Laura! It's so good to see you! I have your herbs."

"Thank you. That's what I'm here for, but I just realized if I pick them up now, I'll have to take them on my walk, and I wanted to stroll along the beach for a bit."

"You're feeling better?" Iva May asked with lifted brows, after thanking the person in front of her and wishing them a good day.

"I am. This is the first time in forever that I've woken up and haven't felt completely exhausted. Like I hadn't slept at all. Except I'm not sleeping."

Iva May nodded. "That's excellent news. I'm happy for you, and I'm encouraged that the doctors were right."

"That's exactly how I feel." She didn't want to pop right back out, but she said, "It looks like you guys are pretty busy in here. Maybe things will be slowed down by the time I get back, and we can chat some."

"I'm sure. This is the tail end of everything. You have yourself a nice walk. That lake breeze is just as good of a medicine as anything else and better than most."

Spoken like a true native, although Laura had to agree. There was just something bracing and refreshing about the breeze that blew in off the lake. Cool and fresh, it felt pure like it could cleanse not just her lungs but her very soul.

"I'll be sure to breathe deep," she said with a wave, and she pushed the door open, the bell tingling above her head, and several patrons looked at her like she might be a slight bit weird.

She didn't even care. It didn't matter what people thought; she realized that more and more as she grew older. She was done trying to follow the dictates of society and color in the lines, doing what everybody thought she should do, watching the same TV shows, the same movies, knowing what all of the social jargon was, and using it correctly. Being savvy with the latest social media, and knowing what the rules were.

None of it mattered. All of it was superficial and fake.

She could see that easily as she raised her girls and heard them talking about the things that were important to six- and eight-year-olds. Things that they thought were life-and-death, that they would just die if they didn't get or didn't have or didn't work out.

How many times in her life had she felt that way?

And yet look at her. Recovering from her husband leaving, she realized that maybe what she thought was the worst thing that could ever happen to her had turned out to be survivable.

It opened her eyes and made her realize that the life she had been living wasn't a life she wanted. Not for herself, not for her girls.

It also made her realize that life was short, and she should be sure to enjoy the things that were important: family, faith, friends. There was a reason why that was a cliché.

But also, there needed to be time in there to do things for others.

Her grandfather had always had an open door and shown hospitality. She'd remembered it all after Dwane had left.

She'd realized that giving to others, food, cooking for them, companionship, or what she did with her job now, giving smiles to people as they picked up dolls that looked very similar to their own families and were blessed with the hours of workmanship that she put into them, was what was really important.

Blessing others. Because she had been blessed.

Sure, her family might not have been the best while she was growing up, but she had so many good memories, good memories that she could share.

She found herself far out on the beach by the time she came out of her deep thoughts, wondering what else she could do, not just to make life good for her and her girls, and not just to bless the people in the shop who actually paid money for the things they bought, but ways that she could give. Ways that she could use her time here on earth so she could make things better for the people who came behind.

Not just liking a post on social media, or signing a petition, or putting a bumper sticker on her car.

She knew people who did all of those things and thought they were doing something to make the world better, but what?

They were all worthless things with no substance and only made a person feel good while exerting little to no effort.

It was the actual boots on the ground, where she touched someone else, with a smile, with a hug, or more. With her time. Giving something valuable.

Deep thoughts from someone who just a week ago was wondering if she would ever get out of bed and go through her day without feeling completely exhausted. And now she had all these big thoughts and ideas about helping others.

She lifted her eyes to where the vast lake met the horizon. Helping others didn't have to be big. It didn't have to be some grand gesture that took the rest of her life.

It could be something small. Something easy. As she pondered what she could do with her limited energy and limited re-sources, she realized that she had picked the wrong direction.

Or the right direction, depending on how she wanted to look at it.

If she wanted to avoid Dwane, just because she didn't want him to think she was fol-lowing him and also because...of that elu-sive feeling—the one she didn't want to admit to—then it might be the wrong direction.

But he was someone she could bless with a smile, with a meal, with a better attempt at conversation when he came to the back room in the shop to sweep up the shavings.

She could work harder at being a blessing. Just to the people she was around, and Dwane was one of those.

So as he came toward her, she lifted her head and put a smile on her face. Not one of flirt, and not a come-hither. Ha. Like she would know how to do one of those anyway. But one of friendliness and a sincere desire to spread happiness.

Maybe it was the wrong kind of smile, because he lifted his hand in a wave, and then his steps slowed until he walked the last five feet to her and stopped with his hands on his thighs, bent over and puffing.

She stopped too, since he seemed to want to talk to her, and she waited.

"It was a beautiful morning for a jog," she finally said, unable to think of anything but the weather to talk about.

"It sure was. Who needs a gym when you've got all of this," Dwane said, straightening and indicating the beach with his spread arm.

"In the winter, you definitely need a gym," she said with a small laugh.

"I'll take your word on that until I experience it for myself this winter."

"So you've decided to live here with your daughter?" she asked, hoping she wasn't stepping over any lines by mentioning his little girl. He hadn't said anything more, and she wasn't sure that maybe she had just been in the wrong place at the wrong time, and he wanted to keep his personal business private.

"I think so." He nodded his head and looked around. "This is gorgeous, of course, but the town is friendly, and my landlord and his granddaughter aren't too bad either," he said with a little grin. Which she returned.

"Your daughter will have friends in mine." Another thing she needed to think about. Although with renewed energy, she felt like maybe she would be able to watch her own children for the summer. Still, she had to work, and she made a mental note to stop in and see Zoriah on her way back through town.

"Yeah..." Dwane said, his voice trailing off. He ran a hand through his hair, which she'd come to realize was a sign of agitation. His breathing had almost returned to normal, and he tilted his head to the side. "You're probably going to think I'm crazy, but the day I ate at your house, I said to the Lord that if you and I ended up on the beach together, I would take it as a sign that I should ask you this. I asked you to walk, but you had to take care of your girls and declined."

"I know. I'm sorry. I hope you understood I really did have to take care of the girls."

"No. It was fine. I totally get that. It's just... It's just I didn't specify that if I saw you on the beach that night. I just said if I saw you on the beach. If we met. And...we've met."

"That's true, we have." He was right. She did think he was a little bit loopy, and she had no clue what he was trying to say, so she waited, trying not to look skeptical or like he was crazy.

"So, you know about my daughter. And that I'm going to go get her the day after tomorrow."

"I do. I hope that goes well for you. Did you want me to speak to my grandfather about giving you the day off?" she asked, uncertain what in the world else he could want to talk to her about.

"No. I've already okayed it with him. And he knows. It's...something else."

"Okay?"

"When I spoke with Dawn, my daughter's grandmother, she said that my daughter, Lizzie, wasn't very comfortable around men. I don't think she's been abused, although..." His voice trailed off yet again, and he looked tortured. Like the idea was almost more than he could bear.

She put a hand on his forearm, which shocked him, apparently, as his eyes jerked to hers. "You didn't know about her. You couldn't protect her. Don't beat yourself up over it."

"I know. It's just the idea that just rips me apart. I did a lot of stupid things I regret. That was one of them. Not that I regret that

I have a daughter, but I regret my cavalier attitude toward everything, and with Shannon, her mother...that I could just waltz in and out of someone's life like that." He shook his head. "Anyway."

"Yes. Go on."

"Dawn said she wasn't entirely sure that Lizzie would go with me. She suggested that I bring a woman friend, my wife, which I don't have, or my mother, or someone who might put Lizzie at ease."

"Had she thought about you staying and getting to know her for a week or so before you took her?" Laura couldn't imagine her own daughters being picked up by a strange man, told he was their father, and then sent off to live with him. That would be so upsetting for them. It made her heart hurt just to think about it.

It would be so much better for them to gradually get to know someone and be able to leave with someone they loved and trusted.

"I would love to be able to do that. Just be there in the evenings after school. Maybe I should have visited her. That just wasn't an option Dawn gave me. Still, I can't do it now, because Dawn is starting treatments for cancer. She actually put them off for a week, and she probably shouldn't since it's pancreatic cancer, and the survival rates aren't that good. But she knew she wouldn't be able to have treatments and take care of Lizzie since she doesn't have anyone to take care of her."

"I see." Laura's sisters lived pretty far away, but she was almost certain that if anything happened to her, her sisters would help take care of her. She would do it for them, if she were able to. She had to get herself fixed first though, since she was hardly capable of taking care of anyone else. If she felt as good as she did today, and each day kept getting better, it wouldn't be long. "I know that that would be really upsetting for my girls, and it makes me sad to think about, but you have to do what you have to do, and it's not exactly your fault that Lizzie's mother isn't taking care of her and didn't inform you of Lizzie's existence."

"I know. I don't think it's probably profitable for me to sit around and try to think about whose fault everything is, so I've been trying to focus on the positive aspects. At least I'll have her in my life now, and I'll be able to provide her with whatever she needs." He sighed a little. "I'm ashamed to say there probably were times in my life where this would be an inconvenience, since I was working pretty hard to get to the top. Not doing that anymore, and I have enough from the years that I did do that to live comfortably and provide for my daughter." He shook his head, probably not meaning to say quite so much. "That wasn't what I wanted to ask you though. I'm not sure how I got off on that, but what I wanted to say is my mom is in Phoenix, and I don't have any sisters. You know I'm new in town, and...you're the only one I really know."

Her brows went up. She should have made the connection immediately, probably. But she hadn't.

Dwane held up a hand. "Don't feel like you have to. Please. I don't want you to feel guilty or like you need to come, because I can do it on my own. Also, I've talked to the lady at the diner, with the white hair…I forget her name."

"Iva May?"

"Yes. Her. She seems like a grandmotherly type and the kind of person that would do anything for anyone, even a complete total stranger like I am. I could probably ask her."

"Oh yeah. Iva May would do it, no question. Even if she had to take off work. She's one of the nicest people I know."

"So, that was you saying I probably should ask Iva May? She won't be put out?"

"I'm sorry." She closed her mouth and tried to think.

She'd been trying to avoid him, trying to make herself more comfortable so that she didn't have to deal with whatever this irritating feeling was that she got when she was around him. And yet, she'd just been thinking to herself that she wanted to find a way to be a blessing to others, not just live her life for herself like she had the first part of it. To be a good example to her daughters.

"I could do it. As long as you don't need to leave until after I drop my girls off at school."

"We could drop them off on the way and just keep going from there. It's about two hours from here."

"Okay. We'll be back before school's out?"

"I don't see why we wouldn't be. But maybe you want to have someone as a backup just in case?"

"I can do that. I was going to stop and talk to Zoriah anyway, about her daughter watching Alessandra and Grace this summer while I work."

"I wonder if she'd be interested in three? I've been tossing that around in my head too. I don't have to work, and I don't think I would keep working just to sweep the shop, but I've really been loving what your grandfather's been teaching me about carving." His mouth opened, like he was going to say more about that, and then closed. "I'd like to keep learning, but I need to do something about Lizzie."

"I can say something when I stop in today. I suppose three isn't that much harder than two, and it might actually be even better, since my girls get tired of playing with each other, and Lizzie might enjoy the company. She's a little older, isn't she?"

"She's ten."

"Alessandra and Grace are eight and six."

"Same age differences my brothers and I had—exactly two years apart. I think they'll get along pretty good, if my childhood is any indication. Although of course we fought like siblings do."

"I suppose it's too much to hope that they wouldn't, but hopefully they have some things in common to be able to get along. If Macy can do it, which is a big if. I'll ask, and I'll let you know when I know."

"I couldn't ask for more. Thank you." He looked around at the beach, then back at her. "Is it okay if I give you my number?"

She nodded, pulling her phone out and thinking about the irony. She had determined she was going to avoid him, and now here she was giving out her number.

After he'd given her his number and she sent him a quick text, they stood, facing each other, with her shifting awkwardly, flipping her phone in her hand, and wondering if there was anything else more to say. She couldn't think of anything.

"Well," she said after what felt like a very long time, and his head jerked up, as though he'd been deep in thought and she jerked him out of it. "I guess I'll go ahead and finish my walk. I'll be in touch later today."

"I'll be around. Maybe we'll run into each other again. It's a small town," he said, a grin on his face and his confident, jaunty air back in place.

"Maybe we will," she said before she turned and started back down the beach.

Chapter 14

The comforter he had ordered for Lizzy had arrived not long after he got back from his jog, and it was the last thing he needed in order to get her bedroom completely finished and perfect. At least as perfect as he could make it.

He hadn't painted the walls any color other than the off-white they were, figuring that if she wanted them painted, she could pick the colors when she got there. Ten was old enough to pick what color she liked, right? There was a dresser, but no clothes. He had no idea what to get for clothes or what she'd come with.

So many things he didn't know, and he was still in a huge amount of disbelief that someone would just let him take a child away with him, even if it was his own.

He hadn't thought too much about Lizzie's mother either. He vaguely remembered Shannon as a clingy and bitingly sarcastic person.

He didn't see much in her, other than the obvious. All his fault and not hers. He'd been shallow and immature, and if he saw her as clingy and sarcastic, maybe she just needed to grow up as much as he had.

She had even more of an excuse than he did though, because as he recalled, she was a good bit younger than him.

Still, he had a room ready, as ready as he could make it, and with the rest of the day stretching out in front of him, he took the camp chair that he bought the day after he'd seen Bill sitting out on the sidewalk in his and carried it down to the sidewalk, setting it up out of the way so people could still walk by but he could observe.

He hadn't even been sitting there ten minutes before Bill came out and set his chair up beside him without saying anything more than hello.

Maybe there was a grin on the sly old man's mouth, and Dwane didn't think it was his imagination that Bill gave an ever so slight nod at his chair, almost in approval.

"So you were jogging on the beach this morning. Still thinking about opening that gym?" Bill asked after they'd sat in silence for fifteen minutes or so.

"Thinking about it. The beach is a great place to exercise though. I can't argue with that."

"Not many people could. But it is pretty treacherous in the winter. Not treacherous, exactly, but cold. Takes a diehard to be out in that kind of weather, and maybe one that's not quite all there, either," Bill said, tapping his head.

"I've been accused of that a few times in my life."

Bill harrumphed but didn't say anything.

A car ambled down the street, tourists from the looks of the rubbernecking. Bill waved anyway, and Dwane followed his example. The folks in the car waved back, smiling, as they continued on toward the beach parking area.

"Must feel pretty odd for you to be sitting around not doing anything on a Monday, with running your business and everything you're probably used to doing. Keeping busy," Bill said casually, grabbing the bottle of water in his chair arm cupholder and unscrewing the cap.

"I admit you're right. I'm used to being busy, but I definitely like the slower pace of this town. I could get used to it."

"If you open the gym, you might be busier."

"For sure. The thought's crossed my mind. It's a negative."

"Yeah. I was in the rat race once a long time ago. It's not really worth it."

"I thought you lived here your entire life."

"I have. But I dabbled in a few other things besides just owning the shop. Better money, and I guess there's the idea to move up and get more and to have more and to own more, but...you lose something when you do that."

Dwane couldn't disagree. His eyes scanned the street, watching for Laura to come walking down. Maybe that's why she was back. Maybe it was just too much for her, or maybe it was because of something else. He kind of hoped and thought that she was the kind of person who wasn't all about the money, but maybe that was more hoping than actual knowledge.

Of course, she agreed to go with him to pick up his daughter; that showed she at least was willing to help out, if nothing else. Maybe that she was willing to think beyond herself and give up a little time to do a good deed.

It seemed simple, but in his experience, there were plenty of people who would have come up with an excuse. Oh, I would love to, but...I can't.

Legitimate excuses for some probably, but not all. Definitely not all.

"So did you raise your family here?" he asked, as the street stayed empty except for a few tourists heading into the ice-cream shop.

"Never had one."

"Sorry. Didn't mean to pry."

"You're not. Just didn't work out for me."

"Couldn't find the right girl?"

"Found her. She didn't think I was the right guy. Maybe she was pretty enraptured with the rat race too."

"Oh." Hopefully that wouldn't be his fate. Although it was a long way from thinking about a woman to actually being with her. He had to admit Laura had been taking up an awful lot of his brainpower lately. He wanted to think about something else. Except maybe he didn't.

His eyes scanned the street again, as though wanting to see who he was thinking about.

"So you think that there's only one right person for each of us, like our soulmate?" he said, just in casual conversation. He wasn't sure where he fell on that. Seemed like in a world of eight billion people, the odds were pretty stacked against a man finding the one person who was his actual soulmate.

He couldn't marry a girl if he never met her, of course, and he'd only met a very small fraction of those eight billion people.

"Nah. Just sometimes, your heart gets hooked on one. Won't let it go. Can't think about anyone else, or just no one else compares, you know?"

"Yeah."

"But maybe that's how you know it's the right one. When she's the one you can't stop thinking about, and the one you want to be with, and the one that makes every other woman pale in comparison or fade away until you just don't notice them anymore."

"Everything you do, you do with her in mind. What would she think of this? How would she react if she heard about this?"

"And you want to do things for her. Make her life easier. Encourage her, lift her up. Praise her. Support her and do everything in your power to see her smile and laugh."

"At me. Not at just any random stranger. Or for any random thing. I want her smiling and laughing at me."

Bill chuckled. "'Course. I thought that went without saying, but maybe I was wrong."

"Well, it's not that I don't want to see her happy. I do. But I don't want to see her happy with someone else. And not necessarily because of someone else."

"Agree."

Just then, Laura exited the secondhand shop, looked around the street, saw them sitting on their chairs, and headed toward them.

"So I guess I figured it would take a woman to lure someone like you into a town like this, and work at a little shop, when you must be a millionaire many times over if you sold your business and it was as successful as you say it was." Bill's words were just as casual as everything else that he'd been saying, and his eyes were stuck on Laura.

Dwane watched her too. "This is going to sound crazy, but it felt like the Lord wanted me here. Does he move men around because of women?"

Bill kind of chuckled. "I wouldn't put anything past Him. His ways are not our ways, that's for sure."

Dwane nodded, wondering if it could possibly be true. Had God moved him to Blueberry Beach just so he could meet Laura?

"So you didn't know her before you moved here?" Bill asked.

"No. I didn't. I guess I came at the same time she did."

"You didn't know each other in the business world?"

"She was in the business world?" Dwane turned his head to look at Bill, wishing they had spoken about this before Laura was on her way toward him. He vaguely remembered Bill mentioning something to that effect before but hadn't thought to ask today for more details.

"I suspect she'll tell you when she's ready."

"I hate it when you say that."

"I say it too much, don't I?" Bill chuckled. "I'm suspecting that it won't be long, and I won't have to say it anymore. She's going to tell you everything you need to know."

"I don't think she likes me that way, but we're going to pick up my daughter together on Wednesday."

"Really? Whose idea was that? Wait. Your daughter is coming here to live?" Bill added that last as an afterthought, almost as though he realized he shouldn't be surprised about that.

"Yeah. I just found out a few days ago. It was a shock to me too."

"Hmm," Bill said, screwing the cap back on his water and standing it in his drink holder. "Kids are a big change."

"I know. I have her bed and a bedroom set up, but I don't know what she's like or what she wants or even how many clothes or shoes or anything she needs."

"You might want to move her into a house. Your apartment's pretty small."

"I thought of that too," Dwane said, non-committal. He liked living that close to Laura. The knowledge that she was nearby, just a few steps away, not that he ever thought he'd need her, it was just the idea. Part of what he loved about Blueberry Beach.

And he hadn't even been there that long.

Plus, it was great to have the shop that he worked at right downstairs.

"I'm not sure she's gonna be able to stay by herself while I work this summer. I haven't gotten all the logistics figured out, but I know that Gavin is willing to work with me, whatever I get figured out."

"That's the hardest thing of all, getting your employer on board. Once you do that, you can usually work things out pretty good,"

Bill said. "There's a bunch of teenagers in town, some of them work at the candy store. You might be able to get them to babysit for a bit, although they're gonna be gearing up and busy with the beach band here shortly. Usually, that's in the evening."

"Beach band?" Dwane said as Laura reached them.

"It's a fun thing that the Blueberry Beach kids and even some residents put togeth-er. Tourists love it, and some of them come back just for that."

"I'd think they'd want peace and quiet on the beach."

"They don't play every day, and you're right, probably some people do want peace and quiet. But most seem to enjoy it. They're pretty good; they do a lot of practicing," Laura added, nodding at Bill. "Hello, Mr. Bill. Not too many more Mondays to take off before the summer rush happens."

"You mean you don't have any days off once the summer rush hits?" Dwane asked, looking first at Laura and then Bill.

"Gotta make hay while the sun shines," Bill said with a grin. Then he straightened out of his chair, grabbing his water. "If you kids don't mind, I'm gonna go upstairs and make myself some lunch." He looked at Laura. "You're welcome to my chair if you like."

"Thanks. Maybe I'll sit for a bit. I have some things to talk about with Dwane."

"Maybe you should invest in your own chair."

"Maybe I will. I'm feeling a little bit more like I can sit up rather than lie down all day."

Bill's eyes clouded a little, as though he were concerned, then the look faded and he grinned and jerked his head before he turned away and went in the side door between his shop and the one next to it.

Laura sat down, and Dwane worked on not watching her.

Funny how she drew his eyes, like the conversation that he and Bill had just had about women, kind of flippant, but so true. He didn't want to look at anyone else, didn't want to think about anyone else or talk about them either. Laura was the only one he wanted.

"Zoriah said that Macy could watch them some, but not all the time. She has some other commitments that will take up her hours and things that she needs to take care of before she goes to college in the fall. She can help us, but not full-time." Laura bit her lip a little, like the lack of feeling in her words was not entirely accurate, and she was more worried than she was letting on about finding someone to help her with her children.

"Well, that's good to know. That will be some help. Did she know what hours?" he asked, running ideas around in his mind that might work out. It was hard, since he didn't even know what Lizzie was like. Maybe she'd be mature and wouldn't need anyone to look after her. Or maybe she'd be clinging and scared.

He just didn't know.

"Mostly in the morning before twelve," Laura said, and she bit her lip again.

For his job, he needed to be at the shop while it was open. For Laura, she could almost work anytime, except she did help pick up the slack when things got busy in the shop which didn't typically happen until the afternoon.

They sat in silence for a while, watching first one car then a second drive down the street. It was hard to imagine the street busy with traffic, although all the locals said it happened. Once school was out and families started taking their vacations, even local families within an hour or two would take a day and drive to the beach.

"I was thinking..." Laura started then trailed off.

"Yeah?" he asked, realizing his mind had wandered, probably because there were so many unknowns in his life, he couldn't figure it out. He was just going to have to wait and see what it brought.

"Well, since we both have kids that need to be watched, I thought maybe we could trade off. You know, where I watch Lizzie with mine, and then you watch Alessandra and Grace with yours."

It was a pretty obvious solution, but he hadn't considered it.

"That's a great idea. I'm good for that. Although, you might not want to commit until you see exactly what we're getting with my daughter. She might be a handful. Especially if she takes after me."

That got a little smile out of Laura. "You gave your poor mom a hard time when you were a kid?"

"Isn't that what boys are supposed to do?" he asked with his best ornery grin.

"We'll see what you think after you have a daughter of your own. Maybe kids think their jobs are to make parents' lives miserable or at least challenging, but when you're looking at it from the parent perspective, you pretty much feel like you can live without the challenge."

"Having children is going to take a completely different mindset. A child. Having a child."

"Yeah. You're starting out at a little bit of a disadvantage, because most parents get to start at the baby stage and step into it gradually. Although you kinda get dumped into that whole feeding every two hours up in the middle of the night no sleep change diaper thing, but as for them actually talking and interacting with you, it happens gradually to most of us."

"I can say I'm definitely not upset about missing the whole diaper thing. Although..." He was upset about missing everything. He hadn't wanted to miss a thing. But he couldn't really blame Shannon. He had been the other half of that couple that had produced Lizzie. He knew what could happen; he just hadn't given a thought that it would.

"If you don't mind, I better get supper going before I pick up the girls from school," Laura said, standing.

"Of course not," he said, also standing, feeling restless, which probably had to do with his nervousness of meeting his daughter, bringing her home, wondering what she would think of him. "We're still a go for Wednesday?" he asked, more because he was nervous than because he wanted to make sure that she hadn't changed her mind.

"We sure are. Is there anything in particular you'd like me to bring?" There was polite curiosity in her gaze, although there was more color in her cheeks, and maybe it was just his imagination, but there seemed to be a flicker of interest slipping across her face as well.

"Thanks for asking. Just your presence will be helpful. I appreciate you being willing to go."

"Of course. I hope I'm some benefit to you."

They started across the street together, and he shoved the hand that wasn't holding his chair into his pocket, giving himself the same argument that his daughter was coming into his life, this wasn't the time to be pursuing a relationship with his intriguing neighbor and coworker.

When they walked around the building and reached the back door, he opened it for her, and she murmured, "Thank you."

"See you tomorrow," he said as she stopped and looked over her shoulder before entering the downstairs portion of her apartment.

"You will. Have a good evening."

He watched her walk through the door, graceful and magnetic to him. He didn't even understand why. There was just something about her. Maybe her calm confidence and how that didn't quite match with the tiredness that seemed to be fading each day.

She still hadn't told him about it, but maybe she would.

Chapter 15

Laura and her girls walked out the back door as she sent the text off to Dwane, letting him know that they were ready and outside.

She could have saved the energy, because as she looked up, there was a sporty-looking vehicle rumbling beside the sidewalk just in front of the door, and she recognized him in the driver seat.

"This looks like our ride, girls."

"Whoa!" Alessandra said, walking slowly around, her eyes bugging out at the fancy car in front of them. It was true. The car

Dwane was driving was much newer and shinier and sportier than anything she'd ever driven. They could have afforded a nice car for her, something sporty and flashy, but she'd never been interested. As long as it started and the heater worked. The radio, too. She really couldn't ask for more.

This. This car was a luxury.

She wasn't sure what she thought of that. She'd spent her time in the fast lane and hadn't been overly impressed with the things it offered. She'd learned they really weren't important. She understood people who thought they were.

She had outgrown that stage of her life and had gotten into the stage where family and friends and a safe place and loyalty topped her list of things that were important.

"This is what Mr. Dwane drives?" Alessandra said, having stopped beside the car with her mouth open and not moved.

"It looks like a spaceship," Grace said, eyeing the car. "Do we have to wear helmets?" she asked, and Laura chuckled to herself. They had just watched a space documentary, and everyone had been wearing helmets. No wonder her little brain had gone to that immediately.

"No. It's a car just like any other. You're going to have to sit in this," Laura held up her car seat, "and you have to wear a seat belt, of course."

"I thought a helmet would be fun," Grace murmured, walking slowly around the car.

Dwane had gotten out and was grinning at them over the top of the low car. "I hope it's okay. It's the only vehicle I own."

"It's fine. The girls just have never ridden in anything this fancy before. They're kind of awed by it, I think."

"How fast does it go?" Alessandra asked.

"I think that's something I'll need to talk to you about when your mom's not around," Dwane said with a wink.

"I think if you can't say it when I am around, you better not say it when I'm not," Laura said, only half joking. She wasn't sure she wanted her daughters to get addicted to speed. Especially as young as they were. She'd have enough trouble with that when they were teenagers.

"Well said." Dwane shrugged at the girls. "You heard your mom. And I think she's wise. Don't keep secrets from her."

Laura grinned, appreciating the backup. It was something that had been missing in her marriage and in the parenting that she did with Christian. Sometimes, it felt like he went out of his way to disregard what she said and do the opposite. It made it tempting for her to do the same to him, although that didn't make it right, and she tried to resist the urge.

Most of the time, she was successful.

All of the time, she had the best interests of her children at heart.

She got the car seat in it and got Grace buckled while Dwane opened the door for Alessandra and helped her in.

Laura opened the front passenger door and sank down into the seat. "Okay. I can get used to this." It felt like she was cradled in warm, loving arms as the seat seemed to float around her, soft and perfect.

"I was thinking of getting rid of it. It's not very practical for Michigan winters."

"It's not. Can't disagree with you there. Although, you'd be comfortable while you were stuck alongside the road," Laura said, smirking.

"True."

"How much did it cost?" Alessandra asked, causing Laura to feel her cheeks heat.

"Alessandra!" she admonished.

"It's okay. They're kids, and they're curious. Although that seems like a pretty interesting question for an eight-year-old."

"I think when you own your own business, kids pick up on that pretty quickly. We've always talked business around them, and they've got that mindset."

At his surprised look, she realized she'd never said anything to him about being in business with her husband. More to avoid talking about her ex than talking about her business.

"You're talking about The Little People shop?" he asked hesitantly.

She took a breath. "No. My husband and I had a business together dealing with online payments and the equipment people use for that."

"You're still a part of it?"

"No. He…bought me out, although I didn't get nearly what my share was worth. I was too tired to fight." She didn't mean for her tone to not invite questions, but she didn't want to talk about her ex and those issues. That was part of why she had moved to Blueberry Beach. To get away from the drama and stress.

She moved the conversation back to the car and they talked a bit about it with Dwane telling them exactly how much he paid for it, and what all it could do, even showing them a few things. And before Laura knew it, they were at the school and the girls were jumping out.

"I wish I could bring this to show-and-tell," Alessandra said as she got out.

"Can we ride home in it?" Grace asked.

"Maybe. We might stop here and get you on our way home. If not today, some other time for sure."

"Yay!" Grace said, and then she slammed her door with a wave to Laura, and she and her sister held hands as they walked up the walk and into the school building.

Dwane watched them for a minute before he turned to Laura. "They seem to get along pretty well. I can't imagine growing up without my brothers."

"I know. I'm so glad they have each other."

Then she realized what he must be thinking. "But if you're an only child, as Lizzie is, you're used to that. And you can't imagine anything else. You get special attention from your parents, or parent, and there's all kinds of perks that go with that."

"You're right. It just seems a little sad to me to not have a brother or something, even someone to fight with."

"You learn a lot of life lessons from your siblings, that's for sure," Laura agreed as they pulled out of the school and onto the road.

"You seem like you're feeling a lot better. Just a week and I can see a big difference in you."

"For sure. Even though I'm still tired, I have so much more energy. Almost on a daily basis, I can feel myself getting better."

"Can I ask what happened?" he asked hesitantly, like he wasn't sure they knew each other well enough to ask that.

She blew out a breath, looking out the window at the flat Michigan landscape as it flew by, the rhythmic thump of the pavement underneath them as they went over the expansion joints filling the silence.

Finally, she said, "My husband and I owned a business together. We dealt with the tech that helps companies get paid online. We were in the right place at the right time, worked hard, build it into something. But everything was in his name."

"That's not good."

"No. He cheated on me with someone he was working with, and when he left, he got everything. He gave me money—I have plenty, but it's not nearly what my share of the company was worth. I could hire lawyers, and I could fight it, and I might win. But I realized, when that happened, that all I really wanted was my girls. And if I accepted the money he paid me, I got custody."

"I agree they're the most important thing, but that's years of work down the drain."

"I guess I understand that." And she'd made her decision and was totally at peace with it. She didn't care for her ex, but that was for a bunch of different reasons.

Wanting to get the focus off of herself, she tried to think of a way to change the subject, but before she could, he asked, "What about you?"

She looked over at him, then out the window at the flat Michigan fields flying by. "Our split wasn't amiable, and there was a lot of stress involved, and I let it get to my head. I shouldn't have, but he made me mad. And of course, it hurt. I loved my husband. I never thought he'd do that to me. So it was a shock, then of course all the doubts came in, mostly why I wasn't good enough, and all the things that were wrong with me, and I suppose in some ways, I was working harder to prove that I was better. All stupid stuff, but...I didn't know what was going to happen. It was just a lot of stress."

"To say the least. That's tough."

"It was. I guess it was too much, and my body just shut down. I had exhaustion that was so thick and so hard and so deep that it was a struggle to get out of bed and get the kids off to school in the morning. That's another reason I didn't fight anything, I was too tired. And also, I just wanted out."

"I see. So there was nothing physically wrong with you? Did you go to see the doctor just to make sure?"

Laura nodded. "That's what I thought. That surely it was being caused by some kind of physical ailment, but I pretty much submitted to every test they have under the sun, and all the doctors could say to me was 'you just need to let go of the stress, and rest.'"

She shrugged, feeling uncomfortable. No one wanted to show their weaknesses, especially to someone who...who what? She was attracted to? She liked? She admired?

He seemed so confident and sure of himself, and he looked good. Tall and muscular, handsome and successful. He sold his business and made millions. Where she'd been given much less than she deserved and walked away, broken in body and spirit.

They couldn't be more different, at least not in that area, and she felt like a failure. She should have something to show for the years that she'd spent with her ex. Something more than a broken body and a broken heart.

At least her heart was healed. Sometimes she wondered how she could have stood being married to such a jerk for such a long time.

"So I assume you guys got divorced?" he asked, sounding casual. His eyes on the road.

"Yeah. It's been final for a while. He had the money to grease the system and make it go through fast. And like I said, I didn't fight anything. I was just too tired. Although I would have fought him if he hadn't given me custody of the girls."

"Visitation?"

"We were left to work that out ourselves. He doesn't typically ask for them too much, although I suppose he will for a week or two over the summer. I expect him to. Not that I want to."

"Is he unkind to them?"

"No. It's just me being selfish. I hate the thought of him with her and my children and them being a family together when he trashed me and wouldn't be a family with me. They're mine. Not theirs, and I hate the thought that she gets to be their mother. It's just...childish. And I would never tell the girls that. I suck it up and wait until they're gone and then cry."

"That can't be good for the low-stress life you're supposed be leading."

"It's not. I need to get over it. It's just...hard."

"Yeah. I don't really understand that, I guess, but when I think about all the years I've missed with my daughter, her babyhood, her first steps, first day of school...just everything. It makes my back teeth want to grind together, and I want to grab a hold of something. I feel like I've missed out on something valuable and precious, and I want it back, but that's impossible."

Laura nodded. "I guess it's not exactly the same, but it's the same feeling of frustration and helplessness. Just nothing we can do, and we have to accept a bad situation, which is hard."

"Yeah." They rode in silence for a while, with Laura trying to get the thoughts of the business she lost and her ex and his girlfriend out of her head. Instead, she needed to focus on what she had. Her daughters, her grandfather, a job she loved, and her health was coming back day by day.

"Did the doctors give you a special diet or anything?"

"Not really. They just told me I need to be healthy. I suppose at first, they just told me to eat. There was a while that I just didn't have any appetite and had to force stuff down. That's natural too, I think."

"I suppose." Then, almost as though he wanted to lighten the subject, he said, "Do you have any advice for me? I don't have a sister, and I really don't know anything about girls. I certainly don't know anything about raising kids. Do you have advice? Hit me with your best stuff."

Laura rolled her eyes and leaned her head back against the soft plush leather of the comfortable seat. "I wish. I wish there was one piece of advice that made everything simple, but I don't know of any. I just know it's not easy. But it's worth it. You know?"

"I'm banking on it. Although I guess it doesn't matter whether it's worth it or not, there's just something inside of me that says I want my daughter, and I want to do what's right by her. Like a responsibility that I need to pick up and carry. It bothers me that it feels like I shirked my responsibility when I hadn't even known that I had one."

"That's good. You've got the parental instincts, and you haven't even laid eyes on your daughter yet. I guess some men never get them." She didn't think her voice was bitter when she said that. But she felt a little bitter in her heart. Her ex was one of those people, one who never really got the daddy instinct.

His fingers tapped on the steering wheel, and she tried to think of something she could do to diffuse his nervousness.

"Would it make things a little easier for you if I say that if you think you need it, you're welcome to come to supper tonight?" she asked.

He glanced over at her, his brows drawn like he wasn't sure what was going on.

"I was just thinking, if things seem stilted and awkward between you two, and you feel like you need a buffer maybe, or if you're feeling overwhelmed or something, you're just welcome. And of course, if you guys are hitting it off and you really get to know each other and there is no need, just don't come."

He finally spoke. "That is so thoughtful of you. I'm floored. Are you sure? You'll have enough food?"

"We'll just make it stretch or throw something else on. I was having hamburgers anyway. There will be plenty." Unless his daughter was a vegetarian, which wasn't outside the realm of possibility. But she didn't say that, because he seemed like he was already nervous enough.

"I appreciate that. I'll take you up on it. We'll come if I need it, and we won't if things are going okay."

"That's perfect. And maybe you can just assume that that invitation stands for any night. Any time you need to come down, for whatever reason, just feel free, okay?"

"That's too generous. You're recovering, remember? You don't need to have two more mouths to feed at the drop of a hat."

"There isn't really that much difference between two mouths and four or six mouths, right? If I'm cooking, I might as well cook enough for everyone."

"Thanks. I appreciate it. Sometimes I think that this might be easier if I had someone with me...if I was with someone, you know, married."

"I guess I wondered why you're not?"

"Well, obviously I spent some time doing things I shouldn't, I wasn't real interested in settling down and just being with one woman. Seemed like there was a whole world full of them, and why would I want to stick with just one?" He didn't look at her but lifted his hands a little off the steering wheel as though to say what can I say?

"That sounds like a sad way to live."

"It is, in hindsight. I wasn't happy with any-thing, but about seven years ago or so, I got serious about the Lord, and that all changed. Since that happened, I've been busy trying to live for Him, which means getting rid of a lot of the bad habits that I had. Then I felt like I needed to sell my half of the business to move here, and there just hasn't been time for women. I suppose though, I'm ready now, even if I am a little late."

She laughed. "I don't think it's ever too late."

"If I want to have a family, kids, I'm pushing the envelope here. People usually do that kind of stuff in their 20s and 30s, not their 40s. I should be having grandkids."

"I think you're a little young for that," she said with a small laugh. "You're talking about yourself like you're over the hill and ready for retirement. You sold your business. You didn't move into an old folks' home."

"Sometimes as slow as life is, it feels like it. Not that I'm surrounded by old folks." He eyed her across the console, with a devilish grin.

"So you thought my grandfather was a young pup?" she asked flippantly.

"Sure is. He'll probably be packing up and leaving and off to see the world anytime now. I better get working on my carving abilities so I can take over his spot."

"I can carve a little. But not like him."

"It'll take me years to be as good as him, but I can see a big improvement in myself already. He told me I could practice as much as I wanted to on the scraps of wood in the bin, and I've actually been doing that at night. I suppose being a parent might curtail my midnight activities though."

"I hadn't realized."

"No. I figured you were probably sound asleep, but your grandfather said I could, so I took him up on it."

The drive went by quickly as they chatted some more about the little people business, carving and painting, and eventually what they each did in their respective businesses that they'd been in previously.

As they got off the interstate and wove around the suburbs of Chicago, his hand started tapping on the steering wheel again, and she fell silent. She'd distracted him for the trip, gave him some backup for later, but there really wasn't anything she could do for right now, and he needed to focus anyway. She'd just make sure that if there was anything that she could do to help, she would.

Dwane's finger kept tapping on the steering wheel, and she didn't need to ask if he was nervous. It was obvious as they motored down a crowded street, with older-looking houses that abutted the sidewalk and no front yards on either side.

The GPS announced they had arrived at their destination as he pulled in front of a house that might have been blue one time, the shutters hanging haphazardly, and big weeds growing up in the six inches between the sidewalk and the rotting front porch.

Dwane looked across her at the house, and she turned to look at him.

His eyes shifted and met her gaze. "This is a terrible time for me to say anything, but I appreciate you coming. And I know my life is going to be crazy or upended at least, and I don't know when I'll have a sane moment again. I just wanted you to know I'd like to be more than friends."

If he had said she had a horn growing out of her forehead, she would not have been more surprised.

He didn't give her any chance to answer but stared into her eyes for just a second before he turned and opened his car door, getting out.

His words had elicited all the unwanted feelings that she'd been trying to avoid.

Not just because he was all wrong for her, but because she'd already been betrayed by one husband, and she didn't ever want to go through that again. Although everything that she'd seen so far with Dwane indicated that he wasn't anything like Christian. It didn't matter. The idea of taking that chance, subjecting her girls to yet another failure, caused her stress levels to spike and made her afraid she might have a relapse with the exhaustion.

She couldn't afford that.

When she had a chance, she was going to tell him so.

She opened her door and got out to follow him.

Chapter 16

Dwane wanted to smack his forehead. What a stupid thing to do. Like he wasn't facing who knows what and should have all of his focus on his daughter.

That was the thing. He pretty much did. But maybe it was also on having a family for his daughter. Which of course made him look at Laura, and his thoughts went along perfectly with the feelings he had.

He'd never been one to sit around. He couldn't run a successful business if he sat around and thought about things for too long. He'd have to make a decision and move with it.

People and relationships were different, and he knew that. He'd experienced it. But thinking about his daughter and that she deserved a stable family, and that's what he wanted to provide for her, and then to have Laura beside him, funny and sweet and considerate and kind, the kind of woman he could see himself spending the rest of his life with, made him want to move on that end as well.

He shouldn't have.

But it was too late. At least he hadn't scared her to the point where she stayed in the car. Her footsteps sounded behind him as he walked up the narrow walk. There wasn't enough room for two abreast anyway, so he didn't wait but walked up the steps and knocked boldly on the door.

He stepped back, then his eyes went to Laura as she stopped beside him.

Not surprisingly, she stared at the door and didn't meet his gaze.

For a couple of minutes there back in the car, he kind of acted like he'd never had a girlfriend before in his life.

He knew that wasn't the way to handle a woman, had known he was going too fast, and had known that she might not feel the same.

It felt like a lot of time passed, and he rapped on the door again just before it opened, and a lady, who didn't look terribly old, stared at them.

"I'm Dwane Hardy. I believe you're expecting me, if you're Dawn?"

The suspicious look on her face faded, and she pushed open the door.

"I'm Dawn. Nice to meet you." She held out her hand but didn't invite them in. Her eyes went to Laura.

"This is Laura Wilson. She's my neighbor and also my coworker. You had suggested that I bring a woman with me since Lizzie is more comfortable with females."

"Laura. Nice to meet you as well."

Laura held out her hand and shook Dawn's. "I'm glad I was able to come. I admire you for helping your daughter raise her child."

"Well, somebody had to take responsibility for her." Dawn didn't sound overly happy and more than a little put out.

"I'm here to take responsibility. I want her." Dwane emphasized the last three words, just in case his daughter was listening. He didn't want her to think that she was putting him out, or was a pain, or anything like that. He wanted her. And he wanted her to know it.

"It's good to see you're stepping in," Dawn said, looking him up and down, making him feel like he was lacking somehow. The sour look on her face made him glad that he wasn't staying in this house and eager to get his daughter out. "You might as well come in. She's got her stuff together, but she isn't going to just go with you. You'll probably have to take her out kicking and screaming." Dawn pushed the door open further and backed into the house.

The furniture was threadbare, as was the carpet, although there was a large big screen TV on the wall. The furniture didn't look too much worse than the stuff in Laura's and Gavin's living rooms, but there was an unkept look about it that contrasted sharply with the shabby but well-loved look of theirs.

The smell of stale cigarettes, moldy dampness, and dirty dog hair seemed to choke the life out of each breath he took as Dawn shoved the door closed behind Laura.

Dwane stood looking at the living room, his eyes roving, searching for a glimpse of his daughter. "I'm eager to see Lizzie. Eager to meet her. Am I scaring her?" he said, excited and eager and wishing that there was a way that he could tell Lizzie that he wouldn't hurt her and that she could trust him and that he wanted only the best for her even though he was going to take her out of everything that was familiar to her.

"She dislikes attention. And she tends to be shy. She's scared of everything," Dawn said, her words clipped. "Lizzie! Lizzie! Get your butt down here. Your dad wants to meet you."

Dwane didn't care for the way she spoke about Lizzie or to her, but he wasn't going to take issue with it since he would be leaving with his daughter soon.

Noting the circles under her eyes, and the way her arms crossed over her stomach, pushing in the faded fabric of her bulky housedress, and the droop of her shoulders, he remembered that Dawn was scheduled to begin treatment for her cancer soon. That had to be weighing on her mind.

A figure appeared at the top of the stairs. Dwane blinked and looked closer, his heart thundering in his chest. This must be his daughter.

Dawn had said she wasn't taking care of anyone else, that she needed Lizzie to go so she could take care of herself during her cancer treatments.

He didn't remember much about her mother, but the honey golden hair seemed familiar, and he thought that's what Shannon had.

But he could see himself in her deep blue eyes and her straight nose that was almost too big for her face. There was fear in her eyes though, and her lips were unsmiling.

She had a hand on the railing as she walked down. She was probably taller than average, as was he, and chubby.

He didn't care what she looked like, short, tall, hair color, or body shape, she was his and that was all that mattered.

That, and that she wanted to be with him. He wanted that. Even if she could never call him dad, or love him, he just wanted her to want to be with him.

"Lizzie?" he said, knowing he probably should wait for Dawn to introduce them, but the lady didn't step forward to do so, and he didn't want to wonder.

The girl nodded but didn't say anything.

"Lizzie, this is your dad. You're going to be going with him as we discussed." Dawn nodded at the suitcases in the corner that he hadn't even noticed. "She's got all her stuff packed up there, and what we couldn't fit in those cases, we gave to charity."

Lizzie's face pinched, and Dwane's heart twisted along with it. Dawn had taken Lizzie's toys? Her things? And just gave them away?

"I wish you wouldn't have. I have room for whatever Lizzie brings with her. Anything."

"Well, it's too late. Right there is all she has left. Other than the sheets on her bed which I'm keeping, and the TV in her room which is mine as well."

The harsh way Dawn was handling this made him want to put his body between the woman and his daughter, just protect Lizzie and help her.

"Hi, Lizzie. My name is Dwane, and you can call me that if that's more comfortable for you than calling me dad."

Lizzie had stopped only about three or four steps down, and at his words, he was concerned that she was starting to get ready to go back up.

So he added, "And this is Laura. She's my...friend. And she agreed to come with me, because your grandmother said that you might be more comfortable with a woman than with me."

It pained him to say it, but he didn't want her to think that he brought someone along because he needed it. Although, Laura's calm presence behind him was an anchor as his emotions seesawed all over the place. Excitement and love that he didn't realize he could feel swelled in his chest, along with irritation and outright aggression toward Dawn who seemed to be treating Lizzie about the same way he might treat a dog. Slightly worse even.

Looking closer at Lizzie's face, he noticed her cheeks were red, and her eyes seemed a little swollen, like she might have been crying.

"Where did you take her stuff?" he asked.

"To the secondhand store down the road a bit. It was all junk anyway. There wasn't anything worth anything that I threw away. Otherwise, I would have sold it." Dawn crossed her arms over her chest and tapped her foot.

"If there's anything that she gave away that you'd like to keep, we can go get it." He looked up at his daughter, wondering if that was what the problem might be.

She shook her head slowly, and his heart deflated. Maybe her tears were because she had to go with him.

Laura stepped forward until she was directly beside him. "Did you have a pet?" she asked. "A dog, maybe?"

Lizzie's eyes opened wide, and they flew to Laura, then they narrowed as she nodded slowly.

"I gave it away too. I couldn't send it with you, and I couldn't take care of it myself. It's not her dog anyway. It was mine. I had it before she came. But I can't take care of it now, any more than I can take care of a kid."

If Dwane didn't know better, he might have said she was all bluster. But she just sounded mean. And he had to admit he had a hard time convincing himself that he needed to be nice to her.

Reminding himself to thank Laura later for the suggestion, he said, "Tell me where you took the dog."

Dawn rattled off the name of a local shelter.

"Text me the address to it." He turned away from Dawn, his hands clenching. "We'll get your stuff loaded up, Lizzie, and then we'll go see if we can get your dog, okay?"

Lizzie backed up one step and shook her head. "I don't want to go."

"We've been through this a million times, Liz. We're not going to discuss it again. I told you, you have to go. Or I'm going to take you to the same place I took your stuff and drop you off there too."

At that, Lizzie's eyes filled up, and her lip trembled. "But I love you. I don't want to leave you. You need somebody to take care of you because you're sick."

Dwane wanted to take a minute to be proud of his daughter for caring about someone else. Especially someone who had been so unkind to her. As he opened his mouth to say something, there was a little crack in Dawn's shell, and he almost thought that her eyes might have been watering too.

It made him realize that it might be hurting Dawn to let go of Lizzie just as much as it was hurting Lizzie to let go of Dawn.

"You're too little to take care of me. I need a grown-up."

"But you can't afford one. I'm all you have."

"I don't have to pay for you and the dog anymore. I can save my money, and I can hire someone part-time for a bit. Now get going. You're holding these people up."

Lizzie shook her head, and one foot went backward to the step behind her.

"Would you be able to come with us?" Laura said softly from beside Dwane. His head jerked to her, wondering what in the world she was talking about. And then he realized she was looking at Dawn.

Dawn? She wanted Dawn to come with him? Was she out of her cotton-picking mind? That grumpy old lady would make everyone in Blueberry Beach miserable. She didn't belong there.

"Maybe you missed the memo, sister. I have cancer, and I need treatments. I can't move away."

"Maybe we could have your treatments moved to the hospital in Blueberry Beach. I've heard they have excellent care there, and many of the doctors who wanted out of Chicago are practicing there, so we have some really great talent."

"I can't afford to move. Everything I've saved is going to go toward my medicine treatments. Just take the kid and get. I'm tired."

She truly did look tired as she put a hand out to support herself against the wall.

"You can stay with us. My grandfather and me and my two daughters. I was thinking about buying a house anyway, but regardless, we have room. We could set you up in the living room, or I can move in with my daughters, and you can have my bedroom." Laura looked up at Lizzie. "Would you come with us if your grandmother comes too?"

Lizzie nodded without hesitation, and Dwane was as tempted to put his arm around Laura and hug her as he was to put both hands on her shoulders and shake her and ask her what in the world she was thinking.

But he kept his mouth shut. He supposed, if he'd been thinking in his right mind and had been listening to the little voice that had been speaking to him since he walked in, he would have known that it was kind of selfish of him to take his kid and leave Dawn to her problems, especially after she'd raised her for the first ten years of her life. That wasn't a very good payment from him, was it?

Maybe part of her grumpiness was the fact that she was sick and scared and losing the little girl that she had loved for the last ten years.

"If you come, Laura and I can share the responsibility for helping to take care of you.

It's the least I can do for what you've done for my daughter for the last ten years."

At his words, Dawn's eyes jerked up. Obviously, she hadn't been expecting his thanks or his consideration.

And if it hadn't been for Laura, she wouldn't have received it either. But how many times did he overlook the things that people did, and not appreciate them, or thank them, or give them the credit they deserved?

It happened even in business. Where employees got overlooked because they weren't loud and didn't announce what they were doing or brag about their accomplishments. He'd seen it over and over. The best workers were the ones who did their jobs to the best of their ability, avoided the office drama, and didn't brag about what they'd accomplished, but instead went out and helped others. Even if it made someone other than themselves look good.

Those were also the ones who normally got passed over, because no one noticed their hard work or appreciated it.

He thought he'd learned some things, but obviously, he still had a long ways to go.

Or maybe he just needed someone beside him, someone who helped him be better. Someone who, hopefully, he encouraged to be better as well.

"What do you say, Dawn? Would you come, at least for the duration of your treatments?" Laura asked, sounding hopeful.

He didn't think a person could fake that kind of emotion.

At least Laura didn't seem like the kind of person who faked things.

"I guess you two must be living together. And I don't think Dwane really wants me." Dawn's mouth pinched. Her eyes were hooded.

Chapter 17

"No!" Laura said, and when Dwane glanced at her, her cheeks were pink. "We're truly neighbors. In the same building, but separate apartments, I promise. Still, they're close apartments, and if he said he would help look after you, I'm sure he will."

"I meant it. And I do want you," Dwane said, knowing it was true. He did want Dawn if it meant that Lizzie would come.

"I don't want to impose."

"You wouldn't be imposing," Dwane said. "I told you, it's the least I can do for taking care of my daughter for the last ten years. And she loves you. And I love what she loves." He hoped that was a true statement. He meant it anyway. Whatever his daughter loved, he would do his best to love and admire as well.

Dawn gave him an odd look over that, but Laura seemed to relax even more beside him, like his words had reassured her somehow, although he wasn't sure how.

"Please, Grandma? Please go," Lizzie said, coming down one step as though wanting to come and tug at her grandmother's hand. "If you go, then I won't be alone. And I can still take care of you."

"You can't do anything while you're in school anyway," Dawn said irritably.

"But your treatments haven't started, and I'm out for the summer. If you come, that solves everything."

"Except who's gonna watch the house? What can I do with it? I can't just walk away from the house."

"We could turn the water and heat off, lock the doors, and I can drive down every couple of weeks to check on it."

Dwane couldn't quite believe that he was trying to talk this crotchety old lady into coming with them. Now he was offering to make a four-hour drive every couple of weeks just to check on her house, which, in his opinion, would probably be just as valuable to society if it were burned down.

Dawn looked at the floor, and he almost thought she was avoiding his gaze because she didn't want him to see her fear, if that's what made her lip tremble and her eyes pinch.

His heart hurt for her, wondering what it would be like to be all alone in the world. Of course she had a daughter, but her daughter didn't even take care of her own child. A person wouldn't expect her to take care of her mother, either.

He had family, friends, and now neighbors who were fast becoming friends in Blueberry Beach. Even though he hadn't been there long, if he were to get sick tomorrow, he was almost certain that Gavin and Laura and probably Bill would do everything in their power to make sure he was taken care of.

In fact, Blueberry Beach was the kind of town where everyone would probably get together and help out. Even if they didn't know him.

How could he begrudge hospitality to this woman?

He was all on board now, but he was still a little bummed with himself for not thinking of it to begin with. He should have.

"Dawn? Let me help you pack your things," Laura said softly beside him.

"It's gonna take a while. You might not want to wait on me," she said, the gruffness back in her voice and her eyes on his face.

"Take as long as you want to. I'll wait all day if necessary."

"Fine. Follow me up the stairs, and I'll tell you what to pack." Dawn brushed by Laura, then stopped. She looked at him. "I don't need no man in my bedroom looking at all my underthings. You stay down here. We'll be down when we're done."

Dwane tried not to let the relief that he didn't have to look at her underthings show on his face. Should he look disappointed? He couldn't quite dredge up that emotion. So he just nodded. "Okay. While I'm waiting on you, I'm going to call that shelter and see if I can get Lizzie's dog back so we can take it with us."

He didn't miss the look that spread across his daughter's face when he said that.

Thankful that he had a dog that he loved growing up and knew exactly how it would feel to someone who'd had their beloved pet given away, he smiled a little at the girl in front of him. So much bigger than he was expecting, older, more mature. She was quiet and looked sweet.

He couldn't believe she came from him.

She was even smiling. Not a huge smile, but her lips kind of curved up, and she looked at him like he'd just offered her one million dollars.

"I'm not sure I'll be able to get her, but I'm going to try," he said gently, hoping with all his heart he could. "What was her name?"

"It was a boy, and his name was Clipper," she said after a pause and look at her gram to make sure it was okay for her to answer him.

Dawn paused when her foot hit on the bottom stair. "Lizzie. You stay down here with your dad, get him a cold drink. You can offer him something to eat, too."

Dwane started to open his mouth to say that he wasn't hungry, but he closed it as he met Dawn's eyes. He got the impression that she wanted Lizzie to spend a little time with him.

He wasn't going to argue with that.

"I would love a drink. Water would be fine," he said, looking at his daughter, who had her lip between her teeth and glanced at his face before looking at her grandmother who nodded.

He felt Laura's eyes on him, and he shifted his gaze.

He loved the little smile that turned her lips up. It made him feel like he was doing okay. He also liked whatever seemed to flow between them. Maybe a little humor at the situation they found themselves in. It certainly wasn't what he'd been expecting on their drive down today.

He didn't want to tear his eyes away, but he did want to go chat with his daughter, so when she started moving down the stairs, he searched Laura's face once more, hoping she realized how much he appreciated her being here and pointing things in the direction that they needed to go.

Who knew what would have happened if he had come by himself. He probably wouldn't have recognized Dawn's gruff exterior for what it surely was: fear and the desire to make sure that her granddaughter was safe.

Frustrated with the bad timing about Laura but eager to talk to Lizzie, he watched his daughter come down the steps.

"I can get you water. It's this way."

"This won't take long. I don't have much stuff I need to take."

Dawn and Laura disappeared up the stairs while Dwane followed his daughter out to the kitchen.

He figured he could sit down, but he leaned his shoulder against the doorjamb, watching her move around, thinking she looked comfortable in the kitchen, and figuring that was because of Dawn. He probably owed her more than he realized.

Not that he would have thought that anybody would owe him for raising a child that he considered his, and Dawn obviously loved her granddaughter.

"So today was your last day of school?" he asked, figuring school was always a safe topic with kids.

"Yeah. We had to go for a couple of hours this morning."

"I see. What grade did you just finish?"

"Fifth." She finished filling the glass up with water, and the ice clanked against the edges as she turned, holding it in her hand. "Do you want to sit at the table?" she asked, sounding uncertain.

Dwane didn't know much about ten-year-olds, but she seemed mature to him. Maybe that's just because she was his and everything she did would seem per-fect.

"If you don't mind, I'll stand unless you're sitting."

She blinked, as though she had to figure out what he said before she could answer. Finally, she said, "Gram told me to stay down here and talk to you, so I'll probably sit down."

He nodded and took the glass, murmuring a thank you, before he walked to the table and pulled out a chair. She went more slowly, like she wanted to see what chair he took, before she took the one across from him at the four-seat table as though wanting to put as much space between them as possible.

"It was awfully nice of that lady to offer to take my gram," she said, her words coming out in a rush as if she wanted to make sure she got them out before she lost her nerve. "I didn't want to leave her. I know I have a mom, but I hardly ever see her, and Grandma is like my mom, and people don't have to leave their moms. I didn't think I should have to leave my gram. Plus, I'm big enough to take care of her now. And she needs me." She said this last almost belligerently like she was afraid he wasn't going to let her be with her gram.

He wanted to ease her mind about that too.

"As far as I know, you can spend as much time as you want to with your gram. Laura lives in the same building that I do. She just has a different apartment, and I know she'll let you be with your gram. That's why she volunteered to have your gram come. She's got a good heart."

"She's your girlfriend?" Lizzie asked, and there wasn't any slyness in her tone.

He appreciated the sincere question even if he did wish he could give a different answer.

"No. But I do like her. I guess I haven't been around her long enough to ask her to be my girlfriend, but maybe that's coming." The subject made him uncomfortable, but it made one side of his daughter's lips turn up, so he supposed it was worth the sacrifice on his part.

"Does she know? That's what Gram asked me when there was a boy at school I liked."

"Did he know?" Dwane asked, his fingers already itching to throttle the little turkey's next.

"He did. He made fun of me. He didn't like me. You probably shouldn't tell her you like her unless you're sure she likes you back."

"How do I know that?" he asked, and the desire to strangle a child had never been stronger. Whoever the little boy was that hurt his daughter's feelings and made fun of her, he wanted to brutalize. Maybe this father thing wasn't going to work out so great for him. He couldn't go around beating up little kids because they were unkind to his sweet girl. He was definitely gonna have to get a handle on that part of his personality.

Lizzie shrugged. "I just asked him. But that's not the best way, because then he knew that I liked him, and he was embarrassed, and so he made fun of me, and after that, he ignored me. I wish I just kept my mouth shut, because before that, we were friends."

"You weren't friends if he treated you like that. That's not the way friends treat people." Dwane tried to keep his voice from sounding fierce. His daughter was talking to him—and he'd been worried she wouldn't. He didn't want to scare her.

Her lips turned back, and she looked down at her hands on the table, and so he added, "A true friend will be there for you no matter what. Even if you say things that make them uncomfortable. Even if you say things that embarrass them in front of their other friends. If they make fun of you, or they laugh at you when you're not laughing, they're not really friends." He took a sip of his water, just because he thought he was getting a little intense, but he wanted her to understand. "But there's a flip side to that too."

She looked up at him, curiosity in her gaze.

"If that's the kind of friend you want, the kind that sticks by you, the kind that doesn't make fun of you, then you should avoid the kind that is nice to you when you're alone and then avoids you or makes fun of you when you're out in front of people." She looked down again, and he figured that was the kind of friend that she'd had. That that boy had been. "Then you need to make sure that you don't do those things to people. If you're a friend, then you need to be a friend all the time."

His partner hadn't been a good friend. Maybe that's why the subject was so passionate in his heart. He and Kevin had gotten along well, but Kevin had always been looking for the next person who could help him. Always cozying up to anyone that he thought would further his career. He'd ditch Dwane in a hot minute if he thought it would help him.

That, and he was always interested in himself. What would be good for him. And he was perfectly fine with Dwane helping him look good, but he never returned the favor. Not that Dwane needed people to be a tit for tat for him; it was just...it wasn't really a friendship if he was doing all the giving and Kevin was doing all the taking.

He realized he'd gone silent, and he looked up at his daughter. "You just made me realize that I lost a friend, and I was kinda sad about it, but he really wasn't a good friend."

She nodded, looking wise, and he wondered if she even really knew what he was talking about.

"So I used to own gyms. The kind you go to exercise at."

"I know what a gym is," she said, and the comment could have been a little sarcastic, but it really wasn't. It was like she was just informing him.

"And I did that with a guy who was supposed to be my friend. But he wasn't the kind of friend who wanted the best for me. He was the kind of friend where he was with me because he wanted the best for himself. And he was pretty eager to go off with other people, if they could give him more than I could." He never actually told that to anyone before. He wasn't even sure if he'd admitted it to himself. No wonder the Lord had prompted him to want to sell the business and to move.

"So you don't own gyms anymore?" Lizzie said, maybe not completely grasping everything he was saying about friends. He felt like it was an important lesson, but he supposed he would have more time to teach her later. Maybe he wouldn't have wasted so many years trying to cultivate a relationship with someone that he was just bound to walk away from.

But... "I guess what it boils down to is a pretty hard lesson. Friendship isn't really about what we get. It's about what we give, and regardless of how people treat us, we need to be sure we treat them the way we want to be treated."

He absolutely didn't want Lizzie to get hurt by any more boys. But being hurt was a part of life. He would rather she grow into a beautiful, selfless woman than protect her from any pain.

At least in theory. He grimaced and deliberately unfisted his hand.

"No. He bought them from me, and so now I have money instead of gyms."

Her eyes lit up at that, and she leaned forward. "You have money?" she asked, and it was as eager and excited as he'd seen her. He was disappointed. His daughter was more interested in his money than him.

Chapter 18

"**I** do. I have plenty of money and could probably buy you whatever you wanted. What are you thinking?" Because he knew she was thinking something.

"Gram could get better health care if she had money, she said. But she didn't, so she said it was more likely that she would die. That's what she told me whenever she told me I had to go with you. That she was probably going to die, and I needed to be with someone who was going to take care of me. No matter how much I told her that I didn't want to leave her, she insisted that I had to go with you." She pushed away from the table a little, crossed her arms over her chest. Like she was protecting herself from him, even though they'd already settled that Dawn was going with them.

"Well, I can't promise miracles," he said. Pancreatic cancer was about the worst kind of cancer he knew of, and he didn't know anyone who'd had it and survived. But he didn't tell Lizzie that.

"Gram said she most likely was going to die because people didn't survive her kind of cancer."

Looked like he didn't need to tell her. Her grandma already had. He needed to have a chat with the lady. His daughter was too young to be facing those harsh realities of life.

Maybe not. Realities were going to be harsh and they were going to be real whether he liked it or not. He couldn't shield her from everything.

He'd never had this deep desire to shield someone from things before. A brand-new feeling. He wanted to protect her from the jerk at school, from her gram's cancer, from anything that might hurt her. They'd only been talking for ten minutes, and already he wanted to kill a little boy and drag her away from her grandma who was mean to her. Put her in a bubble.

He might not survive this parenting thing.

"I can promise you that if I can buy it, Gram will have the very best care I can afford. That's a promise."

She smiled a little, but it was the kind of smile that said that people had lied to her before, and she'd believe it when she saw it, because that's the way her life had gone.

He hated that too.

Who would have known that having children could be so painful? He hurt every time he thought she hurt.

Not a pleasant feeling.

Although, when she smiled at him, even if it was only the turning up of one side of her lip, it did crazy things to his insides and made him feel about ten feet tall and like he could conquer the world.

Having children was probably worth it. That great feeling, compared to the pain.

"I was telling you a little bit about myself, because I was hoping you would tell me a little bit about you."

She shrugged, her head tilted down, like there was something on the cheap chipped veneer of the old table that was somehow interesting.

"What do you do when you're not in school?" he asked, after searching his brain trying to think of something that he could ask that would help him find out more about her.

"I'm here with Gram."

"Do you and Gram do anything?"

"Sometimes she takes me grocery shopping with her. I get to push the cart so she can use her phone for coupons."

He nodded. He'd never used a coupon in his life before. Even when he was building his business, he wasn't poor. His family was firmly middle-class.

His daughter would have been too.

"Isn't there anything you like to do at home here?"

"Gram and I watch TV a lot."

"You have a favorite show?"

Lizzie scrunched up her nose. "Willie the Witch Killer. I hate to miss that one. I hope you have it where we're going. And Tickle My Toenails. Gram likes to watch game shows, and that one's funny."

He'd never heard of either of those two things. Man, it was almost like his daughter was from a different planet.

"We'll have to see what we can do. Maybe we can watch it together, and I can learn about it. I've never heard of them."

"I can bring you up to speed," she said, and she sounded confident again.

"Gram said that you didn't like men and that you probably wouldn't go with me. Why's that?" Maybe he shouldn't be so blunt. Maybe he should beat around the bush. Let her tell him in her own good time. But he wasn't going to force her to answer the question, and he was curious. Maybe it was just men were scary, or maybe there was more.

He did wipe the smile off of her face, and her one eye closed while she looked at him like she was assessing him, and then she said, "Sometimes when I was with my mom, her boyfriends were mean. A couple of them were scary. But they're not like you. You're different."

She didn't say it flippantly, she said it slowly, like she still wasn't entirely sure, and she didn't trust him, but he was happy because it was a start.

"Mean? Like they hit you?" There it was again, for the third time since he started talking to his daughter, he wanted to strangle someone. Any of the mean boyfriends and he wanted to torture them first if they laid a hand on her.

"Two of them did. But not like my friend Lisa at school. Her dad hit her, and she had to go to the hospital. And then they took the dad out of her house and put him in jail. I didn't tell anybody about Mom's boyfriends hitting me, because Mom told me it was a secret."

"It's never a secret if someone hits you. You tell me." He took a breath. "You've got a dad now, and that's my job. To make sure that no one hurts you." Again, he was having trouble modulating his voice in order to not scare his daughter.

She nodded, but he was pretty sure she didn't understand that either. If it had been programmed into her brain that she needed to keep secrets, it was going to be hard to unprogram that. But he was going to try.

"You can tell me anything. Because it's my job to listen to you and fight for you. That's what dads do."

Her shoulders, broad like his and well-padded, came up again. "I guess. I don't really know. Lots of kids I know don't have dads. Or their dad doesn't live with them."

He never thought he'd be raising a kid in a broken home. Or a home that had never been put together at all. It certainly hadn't been in his plan. And Lizzie had paid the price.

"I'm sorry I haven't been here. I didn't know—"

"Gram told me that you didn't know about me. She said Mom didn't want you to know. I don't know why. Mom's never around."

"She must have been around long enough for her to bring boyfriends here that could hit you."

"A couple of times, she took me like she was gonna have me live with her. That was back when I was little. Not too little. After I was in school. I guess little babies are hard, and Mom didn't want to mess with me when I had diapers to change and when I got into everything. But when I was ready for school, she thought she could handle me."

Obviously, Lizzie had been told the story. Either by Dawn or by her mother. He wasn't sure which. Not that it mattered.

"But I guess kids are harder than Mom thought. Which was fine with me, because I like living with Gram better. She's like my mom, only she's my gram too. Which makes it even better."

"She's a really great lady, because she did a great job of raising you." He wanted to say that she hadn't had to, but he was worried that wouldn't come out right, and he didn't want to make it sound like her gram had felt like she had to take her. "It is a lot of work to raise a kid, or so I've been told. Your gram is to be commended for everything that she's done." He hoped that wasn't too big of words, too lofty of a sentiment.

But he was afraid it was when Lizzie shrugged again and shifted in her chair, the look on her face saying she didn't really understand, and she was hoping he didn't ask any questions about it.

He didn't plan on quizzing his daughter. Not today anyway. He supposed, in just the few minutes that they'd talked, he could see times in the future where he would want to quiz her or get names out of her so he could go and thump some people.

He felt his phone vibrate, and he grabbed it, glancing down.

"I'd forgotten about the animal shelter. Your gram just sent me the address. I want to call quick, okay?"

Lizzie's eyes brightened, and she leaned forward again as she nodded eagerly.

It didn't take long for the phone call to confirm that it was indeed the place where the dog had been dropped off and that they would hold it. Although it was going to cost them money to get Clipper out.

Still, he was pretty pleased after he was finished with the short conversation and swiped his phone off.

"We can stop on our way out of town. It's not the way they usually do business, but we should have Clipper with us when we get home tonight."

The smile on her face said everything he needed to know and everything he wanted to hear. He could see why parents spoiled their children, by looking at his daughter's face. Just that smile made him want to do everything in his power to see it again or to keep it there.

"Maybe we should look in the refrigerator and see what will keep and what we need to take with us? Do you think we could do that for your gram?"

He wasn't used to just sitting around. Although, after coming to Blueberry Beach, he'd been doing more of it. It was good for a body. Still, someone was going to have to do that with the refrigerator, and he tried to think of anything else that would need to be done.

Whatever it was, he'd get his daughter to help him. He wanted to spend as much time with her as possible.

He had a feeling this was going to turn out far better than he ever thought it could.

Chapter 19

L ater that night, Laura tiptoed down the stairs from her bedroom and peeked in the door to the living room where she could see Dawn lying on the couch, and as the small creak as the door stopped moving faded, she could hear the gentle snore of the older woman.

Perfect. Her girls were asleep, and Grandfather was in his workshop. Dawn was settled down for the night too.

She was going for a walk.

She had thought the excitement of the day would tire her out, and she was tired, but it was a natural kind of tired. Not the extreme exhaustion that made her limbs feel like there were bricks in her veins instead of blood or that made her dizzy and depressed.

Maybe that's what happened when you did things for other people. Was it so terrible that she was excited about having Dawn in their home?

Maybe it would turn out to be a bad idea, but she couldn't get the happy smile that had been on Dwane's face out of her mind, when Lizzie had kissed her grandmother good night and put her hand in his and gone upstairs with him. It hadn't taken long for him to fall in love with his daughter.

It had been a beautiful thing to see today. She'd been so glad she'd been there to experience it.

Even if what he'd said before they'd gone into the house had shocked her and shaken her and twisted everything that she had been thinking.

She didn't want to do that again. She didn't want to give someone that kind of power to hurt her when they decided they'd rather have someone else and walk away.

Slipping down the backstreet behind the buildings instead of walking on Main Street, she took the familiar path through the sand dunes and came out on the beach.

The moonlight shone down on Lake Michigan, surfing on the broken ripples, reflecting back the light of the stars in countless moving pinpricks.

She supposed the great hulking blackness of Lake Michigan should be scary, but it inspired her. Hearing the waves crash along the shore, knowing the beauty that was in front of her, the mystery, the not knowing exactly what was in the depths of the lake. Loving its changeableness, yet its steadfastness at the same time, and the juxtaposition of those two extremes. They made up the natural body of water that fascinated her.

A breeze blew, a little chilly, and she crossed her arms over her chest, glad she had put a hooded sweatshirt on before she walked out.

She heard the footsteps on the sand be-fore she actually saw the figure and knew it was Dwane.

Maybe it was the line of his neck, the set of his shoulders outlined against moonlight and the lake beyond. Or maybe she'd been drawn out because he was here. Crazy thought, but she supposed it was possible. There was a nagging part of her that want-ed to talk to him, be with him, spend time with him.

She thought he would jog by and go out through the path the tourists used through the dunes.

So she was surprised when his steps slowed, and he turned toward her. She could tell when he saw her, because there was a hesitation of his confident steps, and then they resumed, and she assumed that's when he recognized her. Probably the same way she'd recognized him.

"Hey there," he said.

"I didn't think you'd see me," she replied.

Just to make sure that he didn't think that she was staying there waiting for him, wanting to meet him. Why that was so important, she wasn't sure. Maybe she just didn't want to be forward. Especially after what he'd said earlier. She wasn't sure how she felt about that.

"Didn't think I knew the shortcut the locals used?" he said with a little humor in his voice.

"Well, I know you didn't hear about it from me."

"Bill. He's kinda taken me under his wing, I think. I get the idea he likes me sometimes."

"Bill's bark is a lot worse than his bite. He's got a heart of gold. It's just hidden under a lot of gruffness."

"For good reason, I think."

"Well, then you know more than I do, because I've never heard anything about that."

"I told you he liked me."

She huffed out a laugh and pulled her sweatshirt tighter around her.

"Cold?"

"No. Not really. But you're going to be if you stand here in this wind, sweating the way I'm sure you are."

"I don't think I'm allowed to talk about how I sweat, am I?"

"I think in the dark, it's okay."

"I have to take your word on that. I've never heard that one before."

"It's a Blueberry Beach rule."

"Small towns do have rules of their own, don't they?"

"They sure do. I like them better. Although, I guess I had to experience the others in order to know this is better."

"Understand that." He shifted, and his hand went to his neck, hooking there and rubbing. "I owe you a huge thank you. You have no idea what it means to me to see my daughter in my home, tucked in bed with a smile on her face. I don't think that would have been possible if you hadn't been with me today. I never would have thought about bringing Dawn home, even though I suspected that despite her harsh words and how angry that made me, it was bluster."

"I felt bad for her right away. But I wasn't entirely sure that she truly had Lizzie's best interest at heart until after she talked a bit. I think it was the expression on her face."

"She doesn't have a very good poker face."

"I don't think that's a liability most of the time."

"Maybe not. Probably shouldn't be anyway."

"Agreed."

She tried to calm the swirling of her stomach that had almost whipped up into a frenzy despite the banal nature of their conversation. His words from before he got out of the car and went to knock on Dawn's door ripped through her head.

He wanted to be more than friends. He wanted to be more than friends.

Had that changed?

If it hadn't, what was she going to do?

"You seem like you feel better today. I wondered if getting out might have had something to do with it?"

"I think it was just doing something kind for somebody else. You know, getting your mind off yourself and your troubles, and then they don't seem so big."

"That's true. And I guess the stress that goes with them gets smaller as well."

"It does. I can't say I'm not tired, but it's the good kind of tired, not the kind of tired that makes me feel like there's something wrong with me."

"If it gets to be too much keeping Dawn, you'll let me know. Won't you?"

"Maybe."

"I assumed we'd be taking care of her together anyway. Maybe sharing her like we thought we'd share the kids."

"Yeah. That's kind of how I saw it too. Everything would just work out together, and Lizzie seems pretty insistent that she gets to take care of her gram, so she'll be a help, I'm sure."

"I think so. At least as good as a ten-year-old can."

"It might even be good for my girls. In fact, I'm sure it will be."

"If we're sharing kids and we're sharing a grandmother, maybe that leads me to what I was saying before we got out of the car." He hurried on. "I don't want to push you, if you need time to think or get used to things, but we're going to be working pretty closely together, it looks like, and I'm looking forward to it. Because I do like you. A lot."

She took a deep breath, blew it out. She needed to be honest, in order to be fair with him.

"I like you a lot too. But I'm scared. It was just a little over a year ago that my husband walked out. I know that's not something that you've been through, but it's hard, and it really left me not ever wanting to do that again."

"Whatever you need in order to be comfortable. I can give you references. I can give you earnest money. I'll give you a kidney if that'll help."

She laughed. "Don't be too free and easy with them. You only have two."

"And I only need one."

"Until something happens to that one. Then you'll be coming to me wanting your other one back."

"Nah. That sounds messy."

"Don't give that away. It sounds painful."

"For me. Not for you. I don't want it to be painful for you." He took a step closer, and his hand dropped from around his neck. "So, you're open to the idea of us being more? Because you like me. You said so."

"I know. But I also said I was scared and I didn't want to do it again."

"So could we just be like a little bit more than friends?"

She laughed. "Sounds like you're splitting hairs."

"I just want hand-holding rights. Maybe phone number rights. Maybe..." He stepped a little closer, and his finger came up, brushing her cheek with such a soft touch she barely felt it. She leaned into it without intending to, and he flipped his hand and cupped her cheek. "Maybe, in a long time, not tonight, but some other time, kissing rights."

"That sounds painful."

"I've never had any complaints along those lines. Well, I have had complaints, but they were mostly when I was younger."

"Oh? So you've kissed enough girls to get good at it?"

"I didn't say that."

"No, but you hinted at it. Is that the infer-ence that I was supposed to make?"

"I'd like to say no, but it's probably true. Although, it's also true that it's been seven years since I've had any practice, so I might be a little rusty."

"Okay. I like hearing that a lot better than I like hearing that you practiced on every girl in Blueberry Beach, and I have to wonder which ones are looking at you wanting to practice some more."

He laughed. "None of them are here in Blueberry Beach, and I promise you, I'll warn you so you're not caught unaware."

"Thanks. I think."

"Seriously, I know there's nothing that's ahead of us that's going to be easy. There are going to be bumps in the road with me getting used to Lizzie, and Lizzie getting used to me, and Lizzie getting along with Alessandra and Grace and vice versa, and then throw Dawn into the mix, and the cancer that she's almost surely going to die from, and we've got burdens that would be enough to make anyone cringe and want to run in the opposite direction."

"I'm not very good at running. I've come home in order to stay. Not to run away again."

"And I came because I felt like that's what the Lord wanted me to do. Kind of obvious to me now exactly why."

"Oh? And why is that?" She kinda figured she knew, but this didn't seem like a conversation where one should make assumptions.

"Because of you," he said simply. He didn't hesitate, and he didn't stumble.

"That scares me."

"I know. I guess I can't say I really understand, because I've never been through what you have, but I do know that you'll need some time. Maybe you'll never be ready. But I can say that I've never felt with another woman what I feel with you. I've never wanted to spend all my spare time with someone. Never thought about building a future with someone." He huffed a little, looked out over the lake. "I did business. I was consumed with it. Maybe that's part of the reason I never got married. I slept and ate my business. Sad, but I can tell you now for sure I wasn't spending my time on the right thing. But maybe that was just the Lord making sure that I was available when you were."

That last part almost sounded like a question, and she wanted to agree. Part of her wanted to step forward into this new opportunity. While part of her said that they were moving too fast.

"I've been feeling pretty good the last couple of days, but the doctors warned me that I might have ups and downs. They said it wasn't uncommon to feel better and then crash again. They also said that I would be prone to this for the rest of my life. That any times of hard stress or difficulty could send me crashing down again. And none of them were willing to guarantee that I could crash and always recover. I might end up being bedridden for the rest of my life." She shook her head, shoving her hands in her pockets. "I couldn't get a man to stay with me when I was healthy and fine. I can't imagine anyone wanting to stay with me when I'm not."

"I'm not the kind of man that walks away. I don't look at hard things and decide I don't want to do them anymore. That's when you put your head down and get to work."

She laughed. "I don't want being with me to be work. That isn't what I want either. For sure."

"We don't get to choose what happens to us in our lives. But we do get to choose who we go through our trials with and how we respond to them. Every day, it's a choice. Maybe some days, the choice is easier than others, but that's just what we do. And some people are determined to make the right choice every day, while some people aren't. Doesn't it just boil down to that?"

"I suppose. That seems awfully simple for a complicated problem though."

"I guess maybe I just don't see that it's that complicated. I like you. A lot. I...I might even be falling in love with you. I guess I wouldn't be talking about this if I didn't think I were. Maybe I already am. But it's scary for me to say the words when I don't know how you feel. Not to mention, I don't want to scare you off. But that's how I feel. And I know you like me. That makes it simple. We like each other, let's be together."

He wasn't arguing, not really, but his words made sense to her. Maybe she was just making everything so much more complicated than what it had to be. She was over-thinking things and thinking about what ifs when the what ifs really didn't matter.

She knew one thing that did matter though.

Chapter 20

"We don't even know if our children are going to get along." That was one thing that Laura knew was important. It had to be.

"I grew up with three siblings. We fought every single day. My parents didn't talk to each other and go, 'boy, should we have kids? What if they don't get along?' You just don't have a choice. You know? This is your family, these are your siblings, and you figure out how to make it work."

He was right again. Alessandra and Grace fought every day. She never thought she shouldn't have had them. She didn't get to choose their personality or their gender or whether or not they would complement each other. She just took what the Lord gave her. If God was giving her Dwane, then Lizzie came with him. And they would all have to find a way to get along.

Speaking of, it looked like Dawn came with them as well. One more person to learn to get along with.

"You're right," she finally whispered softly.

"I'm sorry, I couldn't hear that?" There was humor in his voice.

"Maybe you should be closer so you catch what I say the first time."

She was kidding, but he stepped closer anyway, closing the distance between them, moving his face into full shadow as he looked down on her.

"That what you wanted?" he asked, the humor still lurking there, but something else in his tone as well.

"I was kind of kidding, but I guess this is okay. Better."

"So should I give you some time to think about us? Whether you want to try, better yet, whether you want to commit to it?"

"You know…" She put a hand on his abs and slid it around the side, just resting on the hard ridge of muscles under his ribs. "The idea scares me. The idea of commitment, and doing everything again, but being with you…feels right. I'm not scared, I'm not wondering whether or not I'm making the right decision. I know I am. And the closer you get, the better I feel."

"In that case…" He put his arms around her, pulling her close, and she didn't resist, closing the last bit of distance, laying her head on his chest.

Her arms slid around him, and she breathed deeply. He smelled like the lake, fresh and clean and wholesome. Like bravery and character and steadfastness, and a future without fear, one where she would have someone standing beside her, someone she could lean on, who would lean on her. Someone who would face the future with her, whatever it held.

"Is that better?" he asked, and there was sincere curiosity in his tone.

"It is. Honestly. But even though I'm completely comfortable and everything feels exactly right, we're probably moving a little too fast." She let out a breath. Pushing just that much closer to him. "I might not have the energy to handle this."

"I do. And I'll handle it for both of us until you can, whenever that is. And if it's never, that's fine. As long as I'm with you."

She supposed there was no way of knowing whether he really meant it, whether he would really follow through other than looking at his character, and waiting, and seeing. That was part of what made love scary, wasn't it?

A person had to take a chance. They couldn't know how it was going to turn out.

Except...God did know. Dwane seemed completely confident that he was led here for her.

"Wouldn't it be interesting if God really did use Christian leaving me and my exhaustion, which precipitated my need to move back home, and he used all that to bring us together? Wouldn't that be awesome?"

"Do you think for one minute that it was coincidence?" he asked almost incredulously.

"I never thought it might have been orchestrated. I certainly never thought that God would use my divorce for good. I thought good might eventually come out of it, and I might think at some point it was the best thing that ever happened to me, but I was thinking that in a character growth kind of way. Not in a real-life, this is going to make something happen in my life that I never dreamed of kind of way."

"So I'm beyond your wildest dreams?"

"Is that seriously what you heard in all the things I just said?"

"I'm looking for the compliment from the lady."

"Well, this isn't a compliment, but I think I'm falling in love with you, too. I just wanted you to know."

His hands tightened, and his head came down, with his lips touching the spot just where her hairline met her forehead, then he kissed it softly. "Those are some of the best words I've ever heard."

"Some?"

"I'm holding out for the real deal. The actual 'I love you.' Those will be the best. Other than, 'yes, I'll marry you' and possibly, 'I do.'"

"You have big dreams."

"Always have. And I work for them. It doesn't matter how long it takes."

"Years?"

"I hope not, but yeah. Years."

They stood for a bit, just like they were, and Laura figured she'd probably be content to stand like that all night, but eventually he shifted a little and said, "We should head back. Lizzie was asleep when I left, but I'm a little nervous being that it's her first night here. I know, I'm a helicopter dad."

She dropped her arms and stepped back, although he didn't let her hand fall and threaded his fingers with hers as they turned back toward the path.

"I call it responsible and beautiful, and I admire anyone, but a father especially, who takes responsibility for his actions."

"I guess it's because so many dads don't."

"Yeah. I guess."

They took a few steps in silence before he said, "I've been thinking about that empty shop beside your grandfather's shop. It would make a good gym. I've considered investing some money into it and doing that, but if we're going to be together, I want to make sure it's something you're willing to do too."

She smiled, although he couldn't see her in the dark. It felt good that he was talking to her about his plans, like she really was important to him. Even though they'd only just decided that they might try to move forward with something more than friends this evening.

"That's what you're good at. It's what you love. I think it's a great idea. What about the carving? You seem to be good at that as well."

"I've been thinking about it. I think once I get the gym open, I don't need to be there all the time, and I can keep up with the carving in the evenings anyway. I'd like to do both is what I'm saying."

"Sounds like you'll be busy."

"If I get too busy, I'll shut the gym idea down. I want there to be girlfriend time," he said. That was a little bit of a question and then a pause as though waiting for her to disagree with the title he just gave her.

She didn't.

"And there needs to be a family time. Time to take Dawn to her treatments."

"Yeah. I was talking to her while we were getting things ready to go, and she knows that the doctor she was seeing in Chicago will give her a referral to the Blueberry Beach Hospital."

"She said the same thing to me this evening just quickly. I promised that tomorrow I would spend some time on the phone figuring out her insurance, purchasing more if needed, and getting her the very best care I can afford. I've already talked to your grandfather, and I don't have to be in to work until the afternoon."

"I think Grandfather was actually happy to have someone his age moving in. Maybe he and Dawn will hit it off."

"Maybe," he said, but she read in his tone the same thing she was thinking herself. Dawn might not survive. The chances were small for her survival, and it might not matter if they hit it off. It might just make things harder on her grandfather when she finally did pass.

Maybe it was negative thinking, but she felt like she was being a realist. The odds were stacked against Dawn.

"We'll make sure she has everything she needs," she said quietly.

"We will. I can help. I was also thinking about purchasing a house. I think our apartments might work for the summer because we'll be outside a good bit, but I think they'll get pretty crowded this winter."

Her heart sank a little. She didn't really want him moving away. "In Blueberry Beach?"

"Probably. Maybe a little out. It'd be fun to have a lake view, but I guess it's not really a requirement. It's more important to me to find something that will fit our family but will be close. And," he added hastily as though he could feel the pain that went through her chest. A little bit of panic at the idea of their family. "I don't want to push you or rush you into anything. I don't even have to do it. I've been thinking about it for most of the day after we realized Dawn was going to be moving in with us, and as much as I love living on Main Street, it might be a good idea to have a little more room. But I'd want to be married, and I'd want to move with you. So if that takes years then... I guess it takes years."

Her heart pounded, and her breath felt shaky. It seemed like he had everything all figured out, and she was running to play catch-up. She hadn't realized her hand tightened on his until he squeezed, lifting it and cradling it between both of his.

"I scared you."

"A little. Not the idea of being with you, just the idea of everything happening so quickly."

"Forget I said anything. But if you see me looking at real estate online or if there are flyers lying around for open houses, you'll know where my mind is going."

She laughed. "Are you going to pick it out without me?"

"Would it help you make up your mind if I say yes?"

"Let me think about that."

They reached the sidewalk and started in, lifting a hand at Bill who was sitting on the sidewalk outside of his shop.

"Do you know his story?" Dwane asked as they turned the corner and went along the side of their building.

"Not all of it, but I think it was tragic anyway. He seems like such a good man. I'd love to see him find someone who appreciates everything he is."

"I don't know. He seems like he's happy by himself."

"Really? Maybe it's just me that feels like everyone's kind of looking for someone because no one really chooses to be alone on purpose."

"I suppose you're right. Even when I was alone working on my business, I guess you can see I was looking for a casual hookup. Sorry about that, by the way. I'm not like that anymore."

"I believe you. Seven years is a long time to make a decision and stick with it."

"Thanks. I appreciate that."

His phone rang, and she said, "Go ahead and get that. I'll see you in the morning."

Maybe he looked a little disappointed, but he let go of her hand and opened the door while pulling his phone out of the pocket.

"It's my mom. I left a message and told her I had a daughter before I started my run this evening. She's getting back to me."

"That might be an interesting conversation," she said with a grin. Then she sobered. "I better get to bed anyway."

"Text me and let me know you got in okay?"

"My front door is literally right there."

"Please?"

"Okay."

"Good night," he said.

"Good night," she said and turned with eager steps toward her door, surprised that she wasn't more nervous or fearful. But she felt like tonight had been a long time coming, and it was exactly right and perfect.

Even, one could say, ordained by the Lord.

Chapter 21

"Hey, Mom," Dwane said as he put his phone to his ear, cringing a little inside. His mom was a very moral woman, and he knew he'd disappointed her more than once. He wasn't sure whether she was going to be excited or disappointed that he had a daughter.

"I have a granddaughter?" is what she greeted him with. "How old? How long? Why didn't you tell me this? How soon can I come see her?"

"Mom. Mom," he said, trying to get her to stop with her questions. "I just found out last week. I just brought her home. Home to Blueberry Beach, today. You can come see her whenever you want to, and I've gotta warn you, I've got a girl I've got my eye on, so you might as well come and see her, too."

"A girl?"

"A woman. She has two children, and she's divorced. Her husband cheated on her."

"So...are you two together?"

"We live in the same building. I know I told you that I felt like the Lord was leading me here to Blueberry Beach, and I had no idea why. I didn't have a job or anything. I think she's the reason. She's the one."

"The one?" his mother said, and she wasn't questioning him, she was just surprised that he'd finally found the one.

"Yeah. She might not have me. And if she doesn't, I don't think I'll ever get married."

"Sometimes people think like that, then they change their minds."

"Have I ever?"

"You're right, honey. I believe you. And I want to come see my granddaughter, and The One."

"Things are a little crazy around here. I'd better give you some warning." He launched into all of the things that had happened, how he was working in The Little People Shop, and about Dawn and Laura and Lizzie and Gavin, and the idea of opening a business. His mom always had great advice, but he also didn't want her to have any surprises when she arrived. And he knew she would be arriving. From the way she was talking, nothing was going to keep her from meeting her granddaughter and getting to know her.

After they hung up, he stood on the stoop for a few minutes, looking at the dark night sky, thinking about everything that happened this crazy day, thanking the Lord for moving him to this town where his life had been radically changed in so many good ways.

All it had taken was for him to go, having no idea what was going to happen. Just stepping out in faith. That was all it took.

Sunday afternoon after church, Gavin sat with Dawn while Dwane and Laura took their kids for a picnic on the beach.

The food was probably good, although he didn't really taste it.

He spent as much time watching Lizzie with Grace and Alessandra as he did watching the wind blow Laura's hair around her face and admiring her sparkling eyes as she brushed it back and pulled it out of her mouth when it got caught.

After they'd eaten they'd had a water balloon fight, which he could have won easily. Except rather than aiming to win, he'd spent most of the time trying to catch the water balloons.

He'd gotten soaked.

Laura had too, although with her laughter and smiles and how she treated Lizzie like one of her own kids, she'd snuggled herself that much further into his heart.

The girls had helped them pick up the bright pieces of the broken balloons and had run off to the edge of the water, picking up shells.

Laura had put all the pieces back in the container that held the balloons and stood, shading her eyes at the girls who were grouped together and chattered among themselves.

"They're getting along so well," she said with a brilliant smile.

"You seem like you're feeling great," he said, choosing his own topic rather than going with hers.

She closed her eyes and lifted her face to the sun. "I am. I think the fresh air and sunshine and especially..." she opened her eyes and looked at him. "Being with someone who brings out the best version of myself."

"Lizzie does that to you?"

"I love Lizzie. You have an amazing daughter. But I'm not talking about her."

He moved closer, wanting to touch her. He always wanted to touch her. "Hmm...then who?"

She moved into his embrace easily. "You've been good for me. Thank you."

Her words hit him with a warmth she wasn't expecting. "I think of my move to Blueberry Beach in terms of what the Lord did for me. That I met you. That I had a great place to bring my daughter. But maybe He was giving you something you needed, too."

"A man who looks at me and sees someone who's worth his time?"

"A man who looks at you and sees someone he wants to be with for the rest of his life." He forced himself to keep his hands on her shoulders and not pull her closer. "I know I promised I'd go slow, but this man loves you, and I want you to know it."

Her eyes closed and his heart seemed to expand. He'd made her happy – he'd been nervous to say the words – and it made his world brighter to know that he was responsible for the dreamy, happy look on her face.

"I love you, too."

"Scary to say?"

"Yes. But now that the words are out, my chest feels lighter and I want to say them again."

"Go ahead. I don't think I'll ever get tired of hearing them."

"I love you. Thank you for seeing something in me that I didn't even see in myself."

"I see everything to admire in you." He brushed a hand over her soft cheek. "Not that I think you're perfect, or need to be. Just when you're around, I don't want to be anywhere else, look anywhere else, and I want to be close enough to touch you."

He lowered his head and touched his cheek to her forehead, turning his head until his lips touched her skin.

Her scent, fresh air mixed with kindness and compassion, swirled around him.

"Maybe it's not going to take as long as I thought…" she murmured.

"I think the lady is asking me to kiss her."

"I am," she said. She didn't even try to be coy, and it made him think she'd truly made up her mind.

"You've decided I'm not like your ex after all," he asked, lifting his head a little.

"I'm sorry it was even a question," she whispered, her look sincere.

He didn't want to spend any more time talking about it. Not that he was afraid she was going to change her mind, just that he wanted to take advantage of every opportunity he had. Life wasn't as long as he'd thought it was back when he'd been younger and not as wise.

So, he lowered his head, touching his lips to hers and forgetting about the beach and the people on it, the waves and even their girls who still looked for shells just twenty feet away.

Instead, he pulled the woman in his arms closer, deepening their kiss and feeling her arms go around his shoulders, pulling him to her, fitting their bodies together and feeling her curves under his hands.

It was a long time before he lifted his head, lying his forehead on hers and saying, "That was incredible."

She tilted her head, so their cheeks pressed against each other. "Was it? I might need to do it again and see if my brain will work this time."

"The lady's asking me to kiss her again. Sweet." Dwane smiled, not remembering a time in his life where he'd been so happy and content.

"Not asking. She's demanding."

"Maybe I should get her to agree to marry me, first."

Her breath caught and he was afraid he'd ruined the moment. But she moved against him and looked up, smiling. "Is this where I say yes, or do I need to wait for a question, first?"

"Just say yes. I'll take care of everything else," he said, before lowering his head again.

Maybe tomorrow their girls would bicker and fight.

Maybe they'd look for a house together as a family.

Maybe Dawn would fight her cancer and win.

Maybe not.

Maybe Gavin would hit them with a health scare of his own.

It didn't matter.

Whatever happened, Dwane was confident he and Laura would face it all together. As long as she was beside him, they could face anything.

Epilogue

Iva May stood in the corner of the Blueberry Beach diner and watched the festivities around her. In the last few months, Dwane and Laura had bought a house and today they'd gotten married in a small ceremony down on the beach.

Dawn had attended, lying in her special hospital bed, and Lizzie had stood beside her, holding her hand and watching her father with something like hero worship in her eyes.

Gavin's diabetes had been brought out into the open and Laura had him on a very strict diet, and his doctor seemed to think he'd live a long and prosperous life if he allowed his granddaughter to keep caring for him.

Laura and Dwane's wedding kiss had been one of the most romantic Iva May had ever seen, and that was saying something.

Now, as the shop owners of Blueberry Beach celebrated in the small diner, Iva May wondered if it was time to tell her own secret.

Next year would mark eighteen years since The Trio had graduated. The Trio was Iva May's own nickname for Leiklyn, Tiffany and Willen – girls who had been inseparable in high school.

Before she'd left Blueberry Beach for good, Leiklyn had told Iva May that not only had they bought Indigo Manor – an old, Victorian bed and breakfast that had seen its heyday at the turn of the century when wealthy Chicago socialites had escaped the city to relax in its lux interior, but also that she and her friends had made a pact to meet back in Blueberry Beach in exactly eighteen years.

None of the girls had been back.

No one planned to leave forever, but that's what happened sometimes.

But Iva May would bet money that Leiklyn and Willen would be back. Tiffany was more of a loose cannon and not a guarantee.

Regardless, things would be changing. She could feel it in her bones.

And she'd kept her secret long enough. She needed to come clean. Needed to admit to her sin and ask forgiveness for something that was unforgivable.

The idea made her old heart shudder.

She had a letter written just in case her heart couldn't take the stress and gave out before her secret was revealed.

This coming year was going to be a year of big changes in Blueberry Beach. Iva May was sure of it.

Enjoy this preview of Misty Mornings, just for you!

Misty Mornings

Chapter 1

Graduation night, Blueberry Beach High,
eighteen years ago

Leiklyn Weaver, brand-new high school graduate, sat on the knoll by the shore of Lake Michigan, the looming specter of Indigo Inn at Blueberry Beach behind her, with her two best friends in the world on either side of her, staring off into the darkness of the water.

Growing up in Blueberry Beach, there had been plenty of times she had been on the beach at three AM.

This could well be one of the last.

Maybe the beginning of the end.

Commencement meant beginning. She couldn't help but feel that it was an end as well.

Typical thoughts for a recent high school grad, probably.

On her right, Tiffany, a cheerleader and president of the science club, sighed. "I think we're supposed to be happy today. But I've been fighting a weird sadness."

Leiklyn jerked her head to the side. Her friend had been sad? She hadn't had any idea. Tiffany was one of those people who were always bubbly and happy and never met a stranger.

Before Leiklyn could say anything, Willan, who sat on Leiklyn's left, said, "Me too. I mean, graduation was great, and I had fun partying tonight, but there's almost a desperation, like nothing will ever be the same again."

Maybe that's why Tiffany and Willan were Leiklyn's best friends. They'd all felt the same thing, even though none of them had talked about it until just now.

"I did something yesterday. Something crazy," Leiklyn said, not because she wanted to change the subject, not even really because she wanted to cheer them up. Just because she didn't like to be sad. Who did?

Lord knew she had enough bad stuff in her short history that she could end up being sad and depressed for the rest of her life, and she was only eighteen years old.

Hopefully, the next eighteen years produced better memories, not the wretched ones that caused nightmares that would grab her out of a sound sleep, cover her in cold sweats, and give her a deathly fear of hell because she'd done something so terrible God could never forgive her.

Shaking those thoughts away quickly, or they would pull her down, she wiggled her shoulders, bumping both of her friends and giving them an excited grin which they could see easily under the three-quarters moon in the clear night sky.

"You finally said yes when Jake asked you out?" Tiffany guessed immediately.

"No," Leiklyn said, trying to keep the excitement in her voice. She hadn't been interested in dating. Not for three years. Not since Ethan and she...

No more thinking about the bad stuff.

"Guess again," Leiklyn encouraged them.

"You applied for the internship in Amsterdam. The one you've been talking about all year."

"Well, actually I did do that. A week ago, but we were so busy with finals and graduation and all those other things, I guess I forgot to tell you."

"We're your best friends, and you forgot to tell us?" Willan asked incredulously.

"I'm sorry," Leiklyn said immediately, knowing how Willan felt about their friendship. They told each other everything, and when Willan said everything, she meant everything.

She was very particular, dotting all of her I's and crossing all of her T's, and expecting everyone else to do it too. Everyone had their faults, and Leiklyn loved Willan even if Leiklyn's more casual approach to life annoyed Willan.

Sometimes, she wished she had been more stringent.

"It's okay. I guess we were busy. I fell off the wagon on my diet again." Willan pushed her feet out, her hands on the thighs which she claimed were too large.

Willan was a size ten, and she thought she was too big. No matter what Leiklyn and

Tiffany told her, she dieted constantly, always with the goal of being model thin.

She hadn't dated any in high school because she couldn't believe that anyone would actually like her since she considered herself to be "fat."

"I'll start with you again tomorrow if you want me to," Leiklyn offered, although dieting was the last thing she needed to do. She'd been blessed with the kind of genes where she could eat anything and never gain an ounce. She actually had to lie about her weight in order to give blood, not meeting the requisite one hundred ten pounds. That was one thing she hadn't shared with Willan, because she knew it would discourage her.

"Did you decide to move out of your house?" Tiffany asked, knowing Leiklyn had been thinking about it for a while. Ever since her mom had gotten remarried and brought in three new stepsiblings, who seemed to take up all of her time. Not to mention her mom was talking about moving away from Blueberry Beach and down to Chicago where her stepdad's family was from.

All she seemed to want from Leiklyn anymore was to babysit her stepsiblings, and while Leiklyn didn't mind doing it some, she resented feeling like slave labor as she watched them every night after school and every Saturday evening so that her mom and her stepdad could have a date night.

She supposed it shouldn't upset her, since she wasn't interested in having a date night.

"You decided to start dating again," Willan said, almost sounding like she hoped that wasn't what Leiklyn had decided.

"I've done that too, but I'm going to wait until I go to college. And then I'm going to say yes to every boy that asks me."

"Even if you don't really like him?" Tiffany asked, a little incredulously.

"Yep. I'm going to date everyone. The only word coming out of my mouth in college will be 'yes.'"

"See? That's what happens when you go on too stringent a diet. Whether it's food or whether it's boys. You fall off, and you end up gorging yourself." Willan knew what she was talking about, since she'd pretty much done every diet known to man since junior high.

"You don't date, either," Leiklyn said, stating the obvious.

"That's because I'm too fat for anyone to like me. When I lose these flabby thighs and get my stomach tightened up so that there's not a big ripple in it, then I'll date. Although not everyone. I'm only going to date that one special boy—my soulmate. I'll know him when I see him."

Leiklyn said that last line with Willan in her own head. Willan said it so many times Leiklyn knew exactly what she was going to say.

That was one thing about having good friends and knowing them all your life. You could finish their sentences.

"I give up," Tiffany said, and that was typical, too. Everything came easily to Tiffany, and when something didn't, she had a tendency to walk away rather than digging in and trying hard.

Leiklyn probably had the opposite problem. Nothing came easily to her, not finances, not social situations, and especially not her family, which'd been busted up when she was little, and she'd been involved in shifting family dynamics all of her life as her mom hooked up with one man after another and broke up or divorced, and her dad's presence was sporadic.

Leiklyn loved games, guessing games, card games, even hide-and-seek and flashlight tag. Those were the best things about watching her new stepsiblings. They enjoyed playing with her, and she really did love watching them.

The problem was the attitude of her mom and stepdad, who expected her to be their built-in babysitter. All the time.

"I bought Indigo Inn," she said, jerking her head to the large, looming shadow behind her, sure her friends could feel the shiver of excitement that went through her as close as they were sitting together.

"You bought it?" Tiffany said, disbelief in her tone. Tiffany came from the perfect family. Her parents were still married, and they had plenty of money.

She had no idea what it was like to live like Leiklyn had. The unstable family, the constant struggle over money, never knowing whether she was going to have a new dad or not, and when she did, her mom expected her to act like he meant something to her even though she really didn't give a flip. What was the point when he was just going to leave?

"That's what I said," she said, enjoying her friends' disbelief.

"There has to be a catch. Kids don't buy houses. And this one's not even for sale," Willan, logical as always, injected into their conversation.

"So there's a catch?" Tiffany asked.

"Not really," Leiklyn said, stretching her legs out in front of her, putting her arms around both of her friends, and pulling them close. "The township took possession of it because of unpaid fines from the grounds being unkempt. They don't do it too often, but normally, they sell these things to anyone who will pay the balance of the fines. But my stepdad's brother has a friend who's a county commissioner, and I happened to be sitting with him at the wedding reception, and I don't really even remember how we got on the subject, but we talked, he pulled a few strings and talked to a couple of people, and I was able to purchase the house for a dollar."

"But you're a kid?!" Willan said.

"I'm eighteen. And I had a dollar, and I promised to mow the grass and make sure someone took care of the upkeep. I think they just wanted it off their hands because tourist season is coming up, and you know they'll be busy with other things."

Her friends were quiet for a bit, although they both leaned into her. They might not always agree on everything, and sometimes, they had the normal push and pull along with a little bit of envy and the struggle that friends have to get through to get along and accept each other's faults.

But they'd been friends since kindergarten. Even before that, actually, since they'd gone to the same church and knew each other before they even went to school.

It was hard to break bonds like that. None of them had any desire to.

"That's brilliant," Tiffany said, and she didn't sound the slightest bit jealous or upset. In fact, she sounded impressed. "I would never have thought of buying a house."

"It's not a house. It used to be a hotel. It's called Indigo Inn at Blueberry Beach, and there must be something like twenty bedrooms in it. Plus a ballroom. Plus...all kinds of stuff, I've heard." Willan knew everything about everything, and if anyone would know what was inside the house, she would.

"I haven't been in it yet, because I do have to cough up the money for the closing, to pay the lawyers and all those fees for the title transfers and, I don't know, whatever happens when someone buys a house. It's set for next month, and I need to come up with almost two thousand dollars."

"I have one thousand dollars in my savings account. I was going to use it to travel around a little bit the week before I go to college, but...if you let me in on the house, I'll give you the money." Tiffany ran a hand down her long leg as though making sure there was no sand stuck to her skin.

Leiklyn didn't have to think about that very long. Why wouldn't she want her best friend on the deed with her? "You're in."

"I just have a couple hundred dollars. I was saving so I could buy all the things I need to start the air fryer diet plan, but if you let me in, I'll give it to you. And I'll see if I can get some more."

"That's enough. It's not really about how much we give, it's about giving what we can," Leiklyn said, not wanting Willan to feel bad because Tiffany had more money than either one of them. It irritated her sometimes, but Tiffany was never unkind about it. "I think between the three of us, we can come up with enough to cover the rest. But the problem that I'm having is...who's going to take care of it while we're gone?"

Pick up your copy of Misty Mornings by Jessie Gussman today!